Critical Acclaim for *Whompyjawed*

"It's reason for celebration when a fresh new voice enters the ranks of authors. That's the case with Mitch Cullin."

—Dennie Hall, *The Daily Oklahoman*

"Brilliant."

—Andrea Jones, *The Albuquerque Journal*

"With this incredibly touching coming-of-age story, Cullin has mirrored the adolescent experience of millions, and offered a memorable tableau of fast-disappearing rural America . . . and creates some of the most enduring, lovable characters to be found."

—Gail Cooke, *Milwaukee Journal Sentinel*

"It's a world where thoughts flow like an uninterrupted stream and transitions are presented like gifts. It's also a world Cullin understands quite well. This book is the proof."

—Colleen Dougher, *South Florida's City Link*

"Elicits comparisons to such precursors as Larry McMurtry, Erskine Caldwell, or even Sherwood Anderson."

—*Publishers Weekly*

"Readers will not be disappointed with this genuinely talented new writer."

—*Library Journal*

"Mitch Cullin gives us a clear-eyed look at one of those strange and wonderful places where nothing moves on Main Street but the blowing dust when a football game is being played."

—Tony Hillerman, author of *People of Darkness*

"There were *Catcher in the Rye, A Separate Peace,* and *A Fan's Notes*—and now there is *Whompyjawed* the coming-of-age novel for the millennium. In Willy Keeler,

D0424252

wise, confused, and funny protagonist with whom every reader can relate, and has told his story without a single false note. An impressive debut by a writer from whom we now can expect only great things."

—Robert Phillips, author of *Personal Accounts*

"This is a gentle, often traumatic, very touching novel, written with a sure hand in a wonderful vernacular. It belongs in a class with *Catcher in the Rye, The Last Picture Show, The Heart Is a Lonely Hunter,* and Tom Drury's *The End of Vandalism.* Willy Keeler is a young man with a heartbreaking integrity and a sweet gift of zany humor and love that is original and will long be remembered. *Whompyjawed* is real, down to earth, without pretension, and full of small everyday insights and observations that'll fill you with wonder and make you smile."

—John Nichols, author of *The Milagro Beanfield War*

Whompyjawed

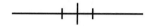

Mitch Cullin

Scribner Paperback Fiction
Published by Simon & Schuster
New York   London   Toronto   Sydney   Singapore

SCRIBNER PAPERBACK FICTION
Simon & Schuster, Inc.
Rockefeller Center
1230 Avenue of the Americas
New York, NY 10020

First Scribner Paperback Fiction edition 2001

SCRIBNER PAPERBACK FICTION and design are trademarks
of Macmillan Library Reference USA, Inc., used under license
by Simon & Schuster, the publisher of this work.

DESIGNED BY ERICH HOBBING

Manufactured in the United States of America

1   3   5   7   9   10   8   6   4   2

Library of Congress Cataloging-in Publication Data is available.

ISBN 0-7432-0208-2

The sections "The Hollow Leggers" and "Ramona with the Black Eye"
were first published in different form by *Austin Flux Magazine*.

For Dad and Brad

With appreciation and love to Charise, Mom, Steve, Jemma, Jesiah, and all my nieces—as well as the Andover-Richmond Gang (Demetrios, Joanna, Ross, Chris, Sarah, and Jeannie S.) and the U of A philosophy grads. Many thanks to Barbara, Bill, Bob, Brian, Carol, Chad, Chay, Dan, Deborah, Edward, Jeff, Kevin, Larry, Mary, Papa Nez, Pete, Scott, Tiphanie—and, of course, Martin and Judith.

Once you hear the details of victory, it is hard to distinguish it from defeat.

—Jean-Paul Sartre

ONE

Game Night

I know some things. A guy can't grow up in Claude without not knowing something about the place. But what I understand best about my town is how it shuts down on game night, how dusk settles over the deserted Main Street with only the blinking of a single yellow light that sort of marks the center of Claude. And with the wind blowing dust and bits of trash along the sidewalks and gutters downtown, not a soul in sight, someone driving through on the interstate could just think a bunch of folks got tired of where they was at and decided to leave for good. Even the domino parlor gets dark and spooky and a fellow would have to strain to see all the posters and signs taped on the plate-glass window. Go by the Dairy Mart on the outskirts, all lit by fluorescent light inside showing it's open for business, but there ain't nobody eating and the parking lot is empty. That's game night. Don't want to see the game? Might as well drive to the stockyard to watch the cattle at the troughs. Might as well walk along the railroad tracks leading from town. Might as well try to learn Hindi from the new owners of the old Trail End Motel.

Not too long ago, when I was still a little kid, I used to climb the water tower on some game nights. I'd sit there with my legs sort of hanging into space, those peeling painted words over my head—*Claude, Home of the Fighting Tigers*—and I'd take in the WPA football field and park from where I was at. Way the hell up there, sometimes the wind was so dry and strong it'd get me tired, but I could see the bleachers on both sides of the field, the big lights glowing down on the grass. The cheering from below would come to me there. Sometimes I cheered too, even though I didn't know who was winning. But I could see the game. And on those Friday nights I knew everybody was there, all the old-timers and cowboys and housewives and kids and people I went to school with, all packed in and around the field, and me, no more than ten or eleven, so far above them that if I had drooled over the edge my spit would've disappeared before ever coming close to the ground.

And I know some other things too. These things I know from no books or teachers, but from the Domino Men with their spit cups and their beer guts and their rough faces, who'd buy me an Orange Crush or a jawbreaker and who'd talk about how Claude was when it was. Few others my age know that Claude once had almost ten thousand souls, though it's got less than half that these days, and that this little dusty West Texas city was a stopover for men trying to get elected as governors and senators. Once Teddy Roosevelt himself whistle-stopped through and made a big speech from the presidential train in front of the depot. Who'd have ever thought that? Another thing, those tracks that brought Roosevelt here was built by the Fort Worth and Denver Railroad when it pushed through in 1887. So this place used to be kind of important, I think. But on game night, like most nights really, Claude is nothing more than a scar widening that stretch of blacktop bypass known as U.S. 287. "The real ass of nowhere," says Coach Bud. But I know better than that.

Three-Finger Talk

Usually Doc Wallace says, "Everybody in one piece, huh?" And we're always quick to answer. He comes into the locker room just grinning, no matter if we've won or lost, with that old black leather medical bag in his hand. And all of us, all the team, we're scattered around old steel lockers or the wood benches. We're still sweaty from the game, geared up or let down, with all our pads and jerseys and personal stuff thrown around.

The Claude Tigers. There's about twenty of us. We got red and black uniforms. Jesus, we're a mixed bag. Even though we got more white than most, we still got several black players and three Mexican brothers. No matter, though. There's no shit between any of us because, one, it's stupid, and, two, we don't win when we're not all together. I make sure that's clear. That's my role in a way. Make sure everyone's pumped. Make sure we're together like a swarm of ants or something like that, like a bunch of monkeys or something. When we win, we all just yell and laugh and stuff, but when we lose, we all feel it together and no one says anything for a long time.

Either way, Doc always wanders the locker room after a game kind of checking us over, looking in our eyes for a concussion or something, sometimes pressing on bones here and there. What I find funny about Doc is his long gray hair, which makes him appear like some old hippie or something. We kid him about that and he takes it fine because that's the kind of man he is, real lively. Some might say jovial, I guess. Sometimes I flash him the peace sign with my fingers and he just shakes his head and smiles.

Tonight Doc goes first to one of our linemen, Harvey, who's

real big and round but not what I'd call fat. Harvey is undressed from the waist up. He's got sweat and dirt on his face because he hasn't showered yet. Sometimes he don't. Three fingers on one hand are taped together with some raggedy bandage, but with his other hand he's busy stuffing his jaw full of Red Man. Doc just stares at him for a bit, shaking his head at the amount of chew Harvey is putting in his mouth, then he points at Harvey's wrapped hand. "Bothering you any?"

Harvey lifts the three fingers so Doc can get a look at them. "Feels fine, Doc," he says.

Doc brings those fingers close to his face, squints his eyes to inspect, sort of bends Harvey's fingers one way and then another.

"Hell," Harvey says, "seventy-two was laying down for me during the second quarter just so he wouldn't have to tackle Willy no more."

"Harvey," Doc says, "you're a case for the books. Peel it and shower. Let me have a see before you leave."

And Harvey nods with that mouthful of chew. Doc pats him on the stomach and moves on. He moves past several of us, sometimes swatting butts, though there ain't nothing weird about how he does it, or touching heads. Then he comes to where me and Lee Haywood, the quarterback, and my black friend Sammy are standing together as we remove our gear. "Good game," he tells us, "all of you. Everybody here okay?"

We nod our heads that we're fine, so Doc repeats himself by saying, "Hell of a good game, boys. I'm proud of you."

"We could've hung thirty more on them, Doc, if Coach hadn't wanted to ease up," says Lee. Then Lee glances at me and Sammy. "Gutting them with Willy," he says, "they was trying to man Sammy. Even I could've hit him all night."

Sammy laughs, flashes a big smile, so me and Doc start to laugh a little too. "All Lee's got to do, Doc," says Sammy, "is get 'em up in the air. I'll be there when they come down."

"I tell you, Doc," says Lee, "it do make quarterbacking fun."

But before I can join in, I hear Coach Slick, our assistant football coach, call my name. So I lean forward some and see him standing outside Coach Bud's office, his thumb jerking toward the open door behind him, saying, "Hey, Willy, Coach wants to see you."

The thing about Coach Bud is that when he wants to see someone, no matter what that person is doing, he had best drop everything and go. Don't matter if he might be getting wrapped by Doc. Don't matter if he's taking a shit or is butt-naked in the shower. He ain't kept waiting by no one, especially us. That's just how it is.

So I go into Coach Bud's office wearing only my game pants and socks, and he's sitting behind his desk in that high-backed, tattered swivel chair. He's as sweaty as the rest of us, maybe more. His dress shirt is stained at the armpits, unbuttoned at the neck, with a wrinkled blue tie loose and dangling to one side. His cheek bulges with a wad of chew. He's got this half-pint wastebasket set on the lap of his baggy slacks for spitting. Thing about Coach Bud is that from looking at him it's easy to tell he was once a player. Even with his thin hair and that heavy hanging paunch, he still runs with us during practice. He's pretty good at showing the line how to block and all. Like if I was to blur my eyes a little, or sort of pinch my eyelids almost shut, he might not look much older than me.

"Yeah, Coach?" I say.

His face is hard, very thoughtful, in a way to where it's impossible to tell if he's happy or mad. He just might break into a funny story or give me some hell about something I done wrong in the game, though he'd be pressed to say what. He tells me, "Shut the door." So I do. Then I turn around again to face him, and he's waving me toward a metal chair in front of his desk. So I go and sit.

I watch as he works that chew a little, spits, then gives me a wink in kind of an admiring way. I've seen him do this before, but it always makes me feel strange. I can't help but shift some in the chair. I glance at the taping table along one wall. Glance at the folding chairs set close to his all-purpose wooden desk. He spits again. I notice the stand-free photo of his wife on the corner of the desk, the old circular-dial telephone, the nameplate made years ago by a shop student that Coach Bud now uses for a paperweight, with uneven carved letters—COACH BUD WARFIELD.

"That was pure-dee football you played out there tonight, son," he finally says. "Pure-dee football."

"Thanks, Coach."

"Know who was up in them stands tonight?"

I shake my head like I don't know, but I got a pretty good idea.

He leans forward over the desk. "Two more recruiters," he almost whispers.

"Where from?"

"TCU," he tells me, "but that don't matter. That's chickenshit as far as I'm concerned. Point is—they're all starting to come in now. And everybody knows what everybody else is doing. That means the big boys are going to be getting serious about you real soon, and that's when I'm going to start sorting the wheat from the chaff. I got eighteen colleges asking about you, Willy—eighteen!"

And now Coach Bud is all excited. His eyes are lit up and I ain't sure what to say or what I'm supposed to say, so I sigh and grin at the same time. I sigh like I can't believe it, like a guy who's worked real hard and gotten the reward, like a guy who knows it was only a matter of time, knows it's bound to happen, whatever it is, and still can't understand it when it does. Sort of like dying, I guess, except in a good way.

"Yessir," Coach Bud is saying, "pretty soon now, we going to start getting down to the nut cuttin'." Then he settles back in his chair, spits once, and stares real seriously at me for several seconds.

My grin becomes odd in my mind. It's forced but honest, and I'm self-conscious of my lips and the muscles or whatever holding them in place that way.

"Willy, it's God-given what you got, son. God-given. I've seen a ton of them over the years—good ones. But not a one that's got it all like you."

I still don't know what to say, I really don't. All I can do is shrug my shoulders. But Coach Bud understands. He gives me another wink. "Well, I'll keep my thumb on the recruiters. You go on now and have some fun."

So I stand. And right as I start to leave, he goes, "One more thing—"

"Yes, sir—?"

"You ain't going in bareback with Waylon's daughter, are you?"

That'd really scare some guys, but it don't me. I know Coach Bud well enough, know how he feels about me, so I just tell him, "Nah, Coach, I ain't going in at all." And that makes him chuckle real hard for a second.

He says, "Well, I ain't so damn sure I believe that, but—"

"I'm not. Not yet anyhow."

"You remember what I've always told you—they's three things that ruin a good ball player quicker than anything else."

Then out comes his three fingers and Coach Bud starts counting them off like he does once or twice a month to me. "There's drugs—" he says and pauses. "There's injury—" he says and pauses. "And there's marriage," he says and pauses. His fingers roll into a fist and he shakes it at me. "So you be careful, huh?"

"Okay, Coach," I tell him.

And as I walk from his office, he mumbles something all soft but I don't catch it, and I'm not sure if it was meant for me to hear anyway. Then I come into the horseplay and noise of the locker room and get slaps on my back and handshakes and good game, Willy, good game, from my team.

'75 Chevy

It ain't much to look at, what with all the circles of rust and those dents, but it's still mine. Stump's my mother's boyfriend, the nearest thing to a father Joel and I got, except for our real father, who's a bum and I'd rather not talk about him, and it was Stump who let me have the truck. He'd had it since high school, says he got his first piece of tail in it, which is kind of gross if you know Stump. Anyway, like I said, Stump's been kind of a father to me and my brother, sometimes he's just like a big kid. Between him and Coach Bud I'm okay. Coach Bud sort of keeps me going with school and stuff, and Stump makes sure I get to have a little fun every now and then. Sometimes Stump just shows up with a six-pack and we go riding in this truck of mine. We go out into the middle of nowhere, sit on the tailgate, shoot the shit about almost anything a guy could think of—girls and stuff, football, sometimes he gets sort of serious and talks about the war, though he don't like to talk about it, and he only does when he's had just a little too much to drink and something reminds him of it, like a flash of lightning over a mesa, or some song on the radio.

When I got the truck, Stump woke me one morning and said, "Come on, son, I've got something to show you." He was really drunk at the time, had been up all night, and his voice was booming around the house. "Don't worry about your damn shirt, come on!" And he took me outside and that uglyass truck was sitting there with the keys in the ignition, a full tank, with the windshield washed. "Don't want you to feel like you got to say anything, don't want you to feel like you owe me or nothing. It's yours." Simple as that. I was sort of still asleep, not even dressed, and he's got his arm around my shoulders. That's the closest I've ever come to wanting to hug him.

Now, after games, once I'm showered and everything, I take my girl Hanna out in the truck. I pull off a feed trail outside of town, park along a patch of mesquite trees. I kill the engine, but the radio stays on—KVRP, the voice of the great high plains, pure country, oldies and good-time hits. It's the best out there like that.

Like tonight, for example, the sky is clear, so bright we can see nothing but stars, not even a single cloud. We are alongside each other on a blanket in the pickup bed. I got on my Wranglers, my letter jacket, my Tony Lama boots. I'm on an elbow looking at Hanna, who's flat on her back, and I'm tracing patterns with my fingertips on her thigh. I got a painful hard-on pressing against my stomach, kind of pushing under the elastic band of my underwear. Thing about Hanna is that even though she's only seventeen, she seems so mature. I mean, I'm nearly two years older than she is, but I sometimes feel like a boy around her. Anyway, she's fine in her Wranglers and school jacket and reminds me of that actress in that movie *Splash,* the one who was the mermaid, except her lips are thinner and her hair is brown. She's gazing at the starry sky while I'm telling her, "We nearly have, Hanna—a lot of times."

"I know we nearly have," she says, "but nearly's not like doing it."

So I go, "If we're going to sometime anyhow, then what does it matter when?"

"It matters because when we do, I just can't be where I have to go home." She sighs, "Mother would just look at me and know."

"How's she going to know? It don't make you bald-headed or anything." Then I laugh some at the thought of her being bald. But she doesn't laugh.

"Because you know how she looks at me when I come in. And if we'd really done it—it'd show. I know it would. It's not like there's ever going to be anybody else—you know I'd never do it with anybody else." But that don't make me feel any less horny. "Besides," she says, "you know when we nearly do it and then don't, I feel just as bad as you do."

"I don't know," I tell her. "Somehow I don't think that's true." She's got no idea how blue-balled I get around her, how sometimes when I drop her off at home my left hand is already unzipping my pants before she's even into the house, how my shorts get all sticky when I'm with her, how sometimes I imagine just holding her down and making her do it right there in the back of the truck.

Hanna snuggles in close to me. She kisses my neck, but I continue the thigh tracing, writing my name over and over. Then we're quiet for a long time, her just kissing under my chin, me fiddling about with her thigh but not writing anymore. And when this coyote lets loose somewhere, Hanna kind of gets a chill through her, sort of absorbs that howl. Then she goes and says the damnedest thing: "A coyote somewhere in the crater of night wails as if a spike were being driven into its soul with muffled blows from the mallet of creation." It comes out of her all dreamy and quiet, just like that, and I'm amazed at how her voice sounded so different from herself when she said it.

"What's that mean," I ask.

She shrugs. "Don't know. It's part of what we had to memorize."

And that gets me hotter for some reason. Just the idea she goes off and reads and remembers something like that gets me all worked up. Another thing about Hanna is how she'll suddenly do something strange that way. One time we was in my bedroom with the radio playing, and out of the blue she starts dancing to this Willie Nelson song—except she's not two-stepping or anything like that. She's running around with her arms out, kicking her legs, very graceful, but not like I've ever seen before. Maybe like a ballet. And I thought she was just being goofy, so I started clapping my hands together like a walrus and arf arf arfing with my voice, and she got so pissed I thought she'd never talk to me again. "Willy," she told me, "you just don't have a sense of art or culture." I guess she's right. But that's what I like about her a lot, she's someone who reads, someone who's got that sense of art and stuff. So I figure it'll rub off on me in the long run.

Now I slip my fingers under the waist of her Wranglers. I do it right as we start to kiss. But, dammit, her eyes pop open. She half smiles her way through the kiss. I'm trying to work the zipper on her Wranglers with my other hand, real cool too, but she brushes my hand away. Suddenly we're both laughing and not kissing no more. She sits up and then, without as much as a word, stands and vaults out of the pickup bed onto the ground. "What are you doing?" I say.

But she just tears off into the night, making ghost sounds as she cuts through the group of mesquite trees. "Woo, where am I, Willy? Woo—"

Man, nothing I don't want to do more than run around after a game, so I shout, "Come back." I say it in a tired way, like I just don't have the energy to move.

I hear her moving away, somewhere in the brush, going, "Come and get me!"

So I try to sound pretty angry. "Hell," I yell, all disgusted and loud. "Come back here!"

"Woo, Willy, woo. Willy!"

Then I can't stand it. I get up, stretch, and then jump from the pickup bed. I go ripping through the mesquites and disappear in a tangle of branches. "Going to get you," I'm telling her. "You just wait, Hanna."

The Hollow Leggers

Our house is about fallen to the ground. It's just this gray, grim crackerbox of a place south of town between Claude and the yawning gap of the Caprock canyon. At night someone can sit on the porch and see the lights of the town off in the distance, and on windy nights this same someone could go on and walk into the darkness behind the house and catch the high, lonesome whistle coming from the canyon. Of course, it all just depends on which way the wind is blowing. When it blows in from Claude I can sometimes catch the stink of the feedlot. That's about the worst smell I can think of. Get one good whiff into my head and it stays with me even after I go inside. Funny thing about that stink is that I could be driving somewhere else, like Wichita Falls or Amarillo, with Lee and Sammy, and there'd be that smell in some other town and dammit if Claude don't jump into my mind.

I've always liked the wind. It don't make me feel sad or scared. It never did. But my brother, now he's different. I mean, he's just a kid, but he gets all jumpy when the wind howls in the Caprock at night. He'll be sound asleep and it'll start, and then he'll be saying to me, "Hey, Willy, I got the creeps." And he'll get me awake. He'll sometimes hang his arm over the edge of the top bunk, and even though it's black in our room I know his arm will be there. "It's okay," I usually tell him. Then I'll find his hand and sort of rub his palm with my fingers. That's all it takes to put him back to sleep.

The thing about Joel is that I really like him. I got friends who can't stand their little brothers, but I'm not that way. Joel's a good kid. He looks up to me and I suppose I got these feelings like maybe a father might have toward him. I mean, he's just a wiry guy with a mess of hair. But that's okay too. I don't expect him to be a football player or nothing. I wouldn't normally say something like this, but I think he's too smart for football. Sure, he's only ten. He likes games and all, except he reads too. He came home from school one day with a brown square of paper from his teacher explaining how Joel Keeler had been given special mention because he'd gone through the required reading list a month quicker than the rest of the class. If it'd been me, I'd have bragged my ass off to anyone who'd have listened, but not Joel. He didn't even show me or Mom that certificate. Mom found it folded in one of his pants pockets when she was sorting laundry. And later she bought a little cake at Sak 'N' Save and this book called *Where the Red Fern Grows* and we planned a surprise party for Joel when he came home from spending the weekend with his pal Chubby.

Mom gathered together her whole gang—Stump, her friend Junie, and Junie's boyfriend Bob—except they got so drunk on Boone's Apple Wine that when Joel finally came through the front door they forgot to scream "Surprise!" or anything. They were all in the living room with the stereo playing, talking like they do when they get drunk, so Joel came on into our bedroom not knowing a thing. He'd walked right past them and they didn't pay him no attention. So I went into the living room and kind of whispered to Mom and she jumped from the couch, which was funny because Stump was resting with his head in her lap.

Mom got the cake and book and we all headed toward the bedroom, and Junie's boyfriend Bob started singing "Happy Birthday" in the hallway and Stump sort of shoved an elbow in Bob's side to shut him up. Then we threw open the bedroom door, and the whole bunch of us shouted, "Congratulations, Joel," which scared the hell out of Joel because he wasn't expecting nothing and didn't have no clothes on because he was getting ready to shower or something. So he grabbed a pillow off my bed and covered himself. We all about busted a gut laughing at the sight of him. Mom nearly dropped the cake. Even Joel thought it was funny, though his face was red as can be.

All the same, it was a real nice evening afterwards. Stump kept telling Joel how proud he was of him. That dumbass Bob kept asking Joel if he felt any older, even though Junie told Bob over and over it wasn't Joel's birthday. And Mom even let Joel have a small Dixie cup of Boone's. It didn't matter that Joel had already read that book Mom bought him, because he said he wanted to own a copy for himself. That's just how he is. It don't matter if he's already seen a movie—if he likes it, he'll see it again. If he checks out a book from the library and enjoys it, he might go and check it out two or three more times in a year.

Sometimes I worry about Joel being around that gang of Mom's, that he'll end up hating them, or that he'll start carrying on like them. But most times he just keeps to himself. He spends some weekends at his friend Chubby's house, and I don't blame him. Chubby's father is a Methodist minister and a real decent fellow, and I think Joel likes being there. I mean, the weekends at our place can be pretty wild. Mom and Junie and Stump and Bob start their drinking on Friday evening before the game and it usually stretches on until Saturday morning. As for me, sometimes I don't mind the partying, sometimes I do. It just depends on my mood, on whether we've won the game Friday night or not. Sometimes I just want to come into a dark and quiet home, other times I want to have a beer or two and join in on the talk.

Some Friday nights, when Mom's working and Bob and Junie are off on their own, Stump and I get beer and drive by ourselves on into the Caprock. We'll be in my Chevy and he'll show me all the dirt roads and secret places he scouted out when he was my age. He'll tell me stories and point out places, like where this old mesquite tree stands alone near a patch of barrel cactuses. "Thomas McKane died there," he told me. "Man was eighty-six. A rancher. Lived by himself and owned about three hundred acres here. They found him laying out under the tree, like he was sleeping, except he was dead. Natural causes. Almost as if he'd decided he'd had enough and was ready to go."

Other Friday nights, usually when the moon is full and sort of appears golden or brown, me and Stump and Mom and Junie and Bob drive into the canyon and find a place to build a fire. And we'll stay out there until dawn, or until an argument starts between Stump and Mom or Junie and Bob. Give that bunch enough beer and there's bound to be a fight. Once when we was all out there, I swear to God, for no reason at all, Stump hauled off and punched Bob. He just popped him in the nose and dropped him. Bob just fell to the ground holding his nose.

"Why the hell you do that?" Junie hollered.

"Don't know," Stump said. "I really don't."

Then Junie went and slugged Stump. I mean, nailed him solid in the forehead, which sent Stump stumbling backwards. Then Mom flew for Junie. And there I was, jumping in between them, and those two women about beat the shit out of me trying to get at each other. When they was done, my shirt was torn, my face was scratched, and Bob and Stump were standing together like old friends, just shaking their heads, holding beers by the fire. Stump was saying to us, "You all need to relax," which about pissed Mom off to no end. And dammit if she didn't pick a rock from the ground and chunked it at Stump. Good thing she was drunk and that rock went sailing over Stump's head, otherwise there'd have been another scene. That's just how it is some weekends.

So now here I am in my truck coming down the dirt trail that leads to our home. It's already past midnight and I got the oldies playing on the radio, and my headlights cut over Stump's blue Ford and Bob's junky sedan, which are parked in the scrub brush and weeds that is our driveway. And there ain't no damn room for me to park my truck in front of the house, so I swing left of the driveway and park along the side of the house next to Mom's clunky station wagon.

When I get outside, as I cross to the porch, I hear swing

music playing on the stereo inside. I hear Mom and Stump and Junie and Bob making their usual racket. I hear Junie going, "Pug, no, wait a minute, Pug—" which is my mom's name. So I pull open the screen door and stroll in real casually, wondering if they'll even notice me. It don't matter sometimes if the screen door slaps shut, or if I got friends with me, that bunch is just in their own world some nights. But soon as I'm through the door Mom is off the couch saying, "There's my big boy!" Then she says to Junie, "Turn the music down!" And Junie, using the big toe of one of her feet, turns the volume knob on the ghetto blaster sitting on the floor. And Mom comes right over to me and plants a big wet kiss on my face.

"Hey, Mom," I say.

She wraps her arm around my shoulders and yanks me into her. "You did good tonight, hon." Then she's nodding at the others. "Wasn't he wonderful?"

Stump's already on his feet, kind of weaving toward me, and he shakes my hand. "Hell of a game, hoss," he tells me.

"Thanks, Stump."

But Junie's too lazy to move. She just stares at me from her chair, looking like she's about to bust through her tight Wranglers and Western shirt, and I see her bleached-blond hair is mussed all crazy. "You sure did good, darlin'," she's saying. And Bob, who's giving me an exaggerated wave with a beer in hand, goes, "How you doing, son?" And it occurs to me right then how ugly Bob is, no matter if he's been drinking or not, with that swollen, whompyjawed hawk-nose sprouting black hair.

Now Stump has taken Mom's arms away from me so he can put his arm across my shoulders. He leads me over to where this big Styrofoam cooler sits open on the floor, the ice all melted to water. Mom kind of staggers along behind us. "Careful, Stump," she says, "my baby might be sore."

"I'm okay," I say.

Stump's pointing at the cooler. "Have yourself one," he tells me, "or two." So I bend, fish around in the cooler hoping to grab a Miller Lite. "Who we got left now, Willy?" Stump is saying. "We got Guthrie next week and then—"

"Lefors," I tell him. I find a Red Dog instead, pop the top, and take a long drink as Stump goes, "Yeah, Lefors. Hell, you boys can take that bunch with your eyes shut, right?" But I shrug because I'm not so sure about Lefors and take another drink. "Shit, yeah, you can!" Stump is bellowing. "And then the playoffs! Then Texas One-A Champs! You boys are going to do it this year, dammit!"

And suddenly the others chime in with slurred agreements, so I just say, "I hope so."

"Hell, yes, you will! And I'm going to make a hundred a game all the way through. Here!" Stump pulls a roll of bills from his pocket, takes a ten from the wad. "Just teaching some of them farmers a lesson about betting on their own boys." He sort of shakes the tenner at me, his fingers creasing it down the middle. "Here—just a little walking around for you, son." And I pause because I don't want him to think I'm greedy or nothing, so he pushes that rumpled bill at me, presses it against my stomach, and I take it from him with a nod and stick it in a pocket. Then Stump steps away from me going, "Hell, I might've told you, Willy, but if I hadn't got my shoulder hurt my senior year, we were headed for district surer than hell, and then—" Everybody starts groaning at Stump.

"You've told it a million times, Stump," Mom says, weaving back to drop on the couch.

"Well, hell," Stump tells her, "I wasn't as good as Willy, but I was pretty damn good."

And Mom and Junie and Bob sort of guffaw. So Stump turns and ambles off toward the kitchen, mumbling something like, "Don't matter nohow with a bunch of losers like you."

Then Junie goes, "Bob, darlin', hand me another one, would you?"

"Shit, ain't you had too much?" Bob complains.

"I ain't had enough!"

So Bob says to me, "Hey, champ, pass me one of them over here."

"I swear you're the laziest thing, Bob!" Junie moans, giving Bob a swift kick in the leg. I get a Red Dog from the cooler and toss it to Bob, who hands it over to Junie. Then Junie goes and pops the top and starts chugging like there's no tomorrow.

"Shit, woman, you must have a hollow leg or something," Bob says, which makes Mom crack up, which makes Junie crack up too, and suddenly there's beer bursting from Junie's lips. And I just leave them like that, all screaming and going on, and head down the hallway because I'm tired and my skull hurts inside.

There ain't much to mine and Joel's room. We got a bunk bed, an old box-stereo with shot speakers. I got me a couple of posters of the Dallas Cowboys and a Coors poster with a fine girl in a pink two-piece swimming suit holding a Silver Bullet can in her hand. Joel's got some stuff on the wall too, like a picture of these Australian wombats or something, which are sort of cute and ugly at the same time, and he's got a poster of some band he and Chubby like but I can't remember the name. Of course, as far as what I've put on the wall, my most prized thing would be my three Tiger team photos, but I guess that goes without saying.

Even after I shut the bedroom door I can still hear them in the living room, but at least it's quieter in here. I begin getting out of my clothes, stripping to my underwear, and I'm doing this in the dark because I don't want to wake Joel. But then I hear him go, "Hey," his voice all groggy, and I can almost spot him stirring in the top bunk.

"I thought you was sleeping," I whisper. Then I go and lean against the bunk because I'm not sure if he's really awake or not. Sometimes he just starts yapping in his sleep and it can be kind of weird. In fact, it can be downright creepy.

"You been drinking?" he says.

"Just a beer is all. What'd you think of the game?"

"Well, we knew you'd win, so Chubby and me picked sides and played behind the stands."

"Who won?"

Joel flops across his bed, arms spread, a sign of defeat.

"Chubby won again, huh?"

"Yeah."

Just then there comes all this commotion from the living room, the screen door slamming, and we hear Junie go, "You son of a bitch!"

Joel leans up. "Junie and Bob again?"

"Yep," I say, going to the window to peek outside.

And there's Bob standing by his sedan with Junie. "Ain't got nothing to say," says Bob.

"You're a son of a bitch," Junie tells him, except it comes out in this stupid high screech.

Suddenly Joel is at my side and we're both watching what's going on in the driveway. Mom ambles down the porch and stops besides Junie with her arms folded, and Bob is getting into his car.

"Where you going?" Junie shouts.

And Bob bellows as he gets behind the wheel, "I don't know and I don't give a damn!" Then he slams the door and cranks the engine.

"Bob! You come back!" Junie screams. "You can't leave! Tell him he can't go, Pug!"

"I can't stop him, Junie! He's just an asshole!"

And Bob has the car in gear. He peels out of the yard toward the road as Stump comes from the house and crosses the porch to where Mom and Junie stand. "Where's he going?" Stump says.

Then Junie breaks down in tears. She drops to the dirt on her knees.

"What's wrong?" Stump is saying.

And Mom is reaching her arms around Junie. "Help me get her inside, Stump! Don't just stand there!"

But Stump bends to Junie's side and yells in her ear, "Now you're drunk! Get your butt inside because I ain't going to carry you!" Except that makes Junie start crying louder now, real wild.

Mom goes and slaps Stump on the arm. "Thanks, Stump, you're a big help!"

"I'm just telling her I ain't in no shape to carry her!"

Mom shakes her head, then she begins pulling at Junie. Then Stump puts his hands under Junie's armpits and yanks her to her feet. And Joel and I watch as the three of them, stumbling, leaning, muttering, shuffle toward the house.

"Think he'll come back?" Joel asks me as we move away from the window.

"Yeah, he'll be back," I sigh. "Get on back up to bed."

Then I almost dive into the sheets I'm so exhausted. But from the corner of my eye I see Joel's outline on the ladder leading to his bed. Except he's sort of just standing there. I'm pulling the sheets in around me, straightening out the bottom with my feet, as he goes, "Can I sleep with you?"

So I say, "Sure."

Then he's climbing in beside me, undoing the sheets I'd already made nice. He scrunches around until he's comfortable next to me. "Goodnight," I tell him.

"Night," he says. Then he goes, "You're cold." And I realize he's right. My legs and arms feel cold. And I lay there for a long time, listening to his breathing get deeper. And when I know for sure he's asleep, I slip from my bed and climb into his.

Beer-Smoke
Hoarse Morning Voice

Mom's smoking a cigarette, propped with her back against the headboard of this queen-sized mattress, and her face shows from the night before, all swollen and pale and kind of droopy. Her scanty nightgown hangs loose on her shoulders. And there's Stump, half-awake, sprawled on the sheets in his underwear. His boots sit all straight and careful on the floor by the bed.

I'm already dressed for the day. I got on my work pants, my Tiger T-shirt from last year, my work boots. While I'm standing in the doorway, Mom is puffing away, all dazed, and we just kind of stare at each other for what seems forever. Then she makes a weary smile and says, "Morning, hon."

But I ain't in the mood for this. I'm tired too, but not the way she is. I'm just tired of seeing them like this in the morning, appearing like two bums or something, messy and undone on that big bed. "Sammy and me are going to work for Mr. Maitland today," I tell her. "I don't know when I'll be back."

And she puffs some more, then she tries to talk all soft but her voice is cracky and doesn't want to come out of her mouth. Finally she swallows hard, coughs a little smoke, and almost whispers, "I might be gone. Got to work a banquet at Lakeside tonight. Can you see to Joel?"

But before I can answer, Stump stirs to life, blinks his eyes at me and goes, "Hey, hoss—" And if I weren't so damn disgusted at the sight of them I'd mention how much he sounds like her, all garbled and scratchy.

"I'm going over to Hanna's this evening," I say, ignoring Stump, who's itching himself under his shorts.

Mom just pushes her shoulders up and lets them drop. "Well, I'll get Junie to look after him."

That's just how it is. "How come you don't get a job here instead of going to Amarillo all the time—" I start, but she cuts in with a heave, a kind of irritated sigh.

"'Cause there ain't no job that pays shit in Claude," she tells me. "And we need the money. That's why."

So I just shake my head and turn and walk out of the room and slam the door.

"Bye, darlin'," she shouts after me, real sarcastic. "See you later." And I just stand outside her door for a moment, thinking of what I can say in return, but then I decide not to say anything because it'd just get nasty after that.

"What's eating him?" I hear Stump say.

"Hell if I know," Mom tells him, and I half believe she knows I'm listening. "He's always been a moody little shit." Then she coughs some, and then Stump coughs some too.

The bed squeaks. Stump's feet plop heavy to the floor. "I got to get home." And then there's silence, and I can almost imagine Mom taking another slow drag on that coffin nail.

T.K. and Jackie

T. K. Maitland is about the richest guy in the county, but some would never know by the sight of him. He comes into town in that dented, sputtering heap he calls Mother, even though it's just a Chevy truck like mine. He's got a sunburnt elbow sticking out over the driver's door, he's driving real slow with the other hand, which is hanging all lazy on the steering wheel, a cigar stuck between them long fingers of his. He's always wearing that soily Stetson and Wranglers like mine and boots with patched holes in the bottom. The Domino Men, who set up in front of the parlor in the spring, call to T.K. as he motors past, "Got us room for one more player," or, "Where you been, T.K.? Get on over here." But T.K. just flashes that mouthful of dirty teeth and says something like, "I'd love to, except Mother's taking me home," or, "Mother's heading somewhere and I'm curious to see where it is."

What I like most about T.K. is that he don't try to act richer than the rest of Claude. He's still got that money but it don't show on him at all. He don't throw his wealth around, he don't buy planes and stuff, he's just another cowboy who happens to own the largest working ranch near Claude. And he's always been friendly to me. Way before I was playing football, he'd have me and Sammy and Lee to come swim at his pool in the summer. Then Mrs. Maitland would cook us lunch, usually something like a hamburger with hash browns, and we'd sit in the shade around that big two-story brick home of theirs just eating, letting the grease drip onto our stomachs. We'd half slobber ourselves silly over her food, then—SPLASH!—we was back in the pool, spitting water, doing Marco Polo or some other kid game.

Another thing, it didn't bug the Maitlands none that Sammy was black, or that Lee's father had once been fired as a workhand by T.K. for stealing a bale of barbed wire. And sometimes the three of us would just show up out of the blue with our trunks and T.K.'d say, "Go ahead. Make yourself at home. Just don't piss in the water." He'd even give us a beer every now and then during them summers. That's the kind of fellow he is.

Nowadays T.K. pushes some work my way on the weekends. It don't pay all that great, but at least it gets me gas and things like that. He's pretty loose. He'll pay me from his pocket and say something like, "You need a little extra? You got a honey on the side that needs some tending?" And sometimes I'll say, "Sure," but most times I tell him I'm okay. It's not that I don't need the dough, it's just that I don't want him to think I'm taking advantage or nothing.

Most Saturdays T.K. stands by as me and Sammy and a pair of old wetback cowboys called Jesus and Lorenzo mess with cattle in the corrals. T.K. chews on this unlit cigar and hollers out what we need to do or what we're doing wrong.

Sometimes Pete, who's the local veterinarian, joins us in his splotched and splattered leather apron. He'll have with him one of those huge hypodermic syringes, and Sammy and me will go about wrestling calves, one at a time, into one end of a holding chute. It's hard, hot, dirty work, with the calf jarring around and tossing as we haul it away from the herd. When we run that calf right into the narrow chute, I throw this lever to trap its neck, and then Jesus and Lorenzo take over and grapple the calf's head up so Pete can move in for the two-step process. With a rubber-gloved hand, Pete shoves a big capsule down the calf's throat, then he strokes its neck until the pill goes down. Then he takes the syringe and injects the calf's hip. And the whole damn time the pitiful thing is bellowing with its eyes all bugged. Sometimes it'll haul off and dump or piss right there in the chute because it's so scared. Can't say I wouldn't do the same. When he's finished with the calf, Pete says to me and Sammy,

"Okay, boys—" which means we got to go get another and do the whole routine again.

That's how it is today. Pete goes, "Okay, boys—" and I open the chute while Sammy shoves on the calf from behind. When the calf finally goes and bounds out the other end of the chute, I join Sammy and we pause to get our breath before heading back into the herd.

T.K. steps to Pete and slaps him on the back, saying, "I'm going to run now, Pete. Make damn sure you don't miss anything."

"I think they're cleaner than a whistle," Pete says, "but if I see anything, we'll hold them."

Then T.K. nods to Pete. Then he nods to the Mexicans. Then he nods at me and Sammy. His face softens some as he tells us, "And you two be damn careful. We don't want any broke arms out here."

"Yes, sir," I say.

"Okay, Mr. Maitland," Sammy says, wiping sweat from his forehead.

Then T.K. comes over to us. He sort of waves me and Sammy close with his hands and almost whispers, "When you finish up, stop by the house and Patti'll fix you lunch." Which sounds real good to me because I didn't get breakfast and my stomach feels about as empty as one of them crushed Coors cans in the bed of Stump's truck.

So Sammy and I say thanks, and T.K. gives us his nasty-teeth grin. And as he turns to leave I see that his son Jackie is leaning nearby on the other side of the corral railing. It's always kind of funny to see Jackie out here, because he don't fit at all. He's a couple years younger than me and Sammy, all skinny and milky-white, though he ain't sick or ugly or nothing. In his own way, Jackie's kind of handsome for his age, and he's a real pal to the girls. They practically wet themselves trying to get a seat by him in the cafeteria, though he don't play sports worth shit. In fact, he don't play at all these days. But he's always dressed nice, and today he's got on a blue knit shirt, chinos, and loafers, like he's going to church or somewhere. All the same, he's okay. I know some of the guys give him a hard time, but I don't. Neither does Sammy. But Lee really lays into him sometimes, though Lee knows I don't like it because T.K.'s always been good to me.

Jackie's face brightens when he sees us in the corral. "Hi, Willy—Sammy."

"Hey, Jackie," me and Sammy say together, which makes both of us laugh some.

"What you need, Jackie?" T.K. says.

"Mom said to stop by before you leave. She needs something from town."

"What now?" T.K. grumbles to himself. Then he puts that cigar in his mouth and starts to climb the corral fence.

"You want me to do something here, Dad?" Jackie asks before T.K. can even get halfway over the fence.

And when T.K. drops down next to his son, he stops for a long moment to look at him. Then he says, with this edge in his voice, "Now, what the hell would you do here, Jackie? This is man's work." Which makes Sammy cock an eyebrow. Which makes me want to walk away. And Jackie's face kind of flinches from the remark. So I glance to where Pete and Jesus and Lorenzo stand by the chute and see that they're also getting the awkwardness, because they're all staring at their feet and not doing anything that'd come close to resembling work. But none of this seems to trouble T.K., because he's already heading toward the big house, speaking over his shoulder, "Don't let him get in the way!"

Then Jackie tries to smile as if it's funny, shrugs his shoulders some, but the hurt shows. Then Pete claps his hands together and says, "Well, let's get at them!" And as me and Sammy go for another calf, I know Jackie's eyes are following me.

The thing is, I feel kind of bad for Jackie. Him being the way he is and all. He's just Jackie, and most of us take him for just that. Those summers when me and the others would go swimming at the big house, we'd always try to get him to join us, but most times he'd go, "That's okay."

Once we got him in the pool for a game of tag, and it seemed like he was having as much fun as us, until Lee went and dunked him and held him underwater for what seemed forever. After that, he pretty much steered clear of the pool when we was there. But sometimes I'd catch him staring out at us from his bedroom window. And even though he wasn't swimming or nothing, he'd be wearing his trunks, just watching us mess around. I don't think Lee or Sammy ever knew he was there, but I did. And he knew I did, because sometimes I'd give him a wave to join us and he'd step back from that window.

I feel bad about something else too, but I try not to think on it too much. It's just one of them things that happens, and afterwards a guy wonders why it did. This thing happened a few summers ago, so it don't eat at me like it did then. I mean, hell, I was fifteen and Jackie was on the phone asking if I wanted to come swim because his folks were in Amarillo for the day. The whole thing seems kind of weird now because Jackie had never called me before, and he hasn't since then. He never wanted to swim when I was there with the others, never had much to say to me at school. He always appeared sort of nervous. I thought he was shy, but Lee thought he was just stuck on himself. Anyway, I got over to the big house with my trunks, and Jackie was all glad to see me. He had a bowl of trail mix, so we sat in the living room and started talking about school, people at school, and we just cut up about girls and stuff. It was like we were the best of friends. And I remember thinking, "This guy ain't so bad."

Then we was out in the pool and it was getting dark outside. Jackie kicked around some, going under with these goggles and snorkel. I did dives off the board. Then he was doing dives too. We took turns making cannonballs until we had the pool rocking. We kept doing those cannonballs, and the pool got all wavy, like a real storm or something. And soon we'd created a regular disaster, with the water crashing high past the pool edges.

So me and Jackie floated in the deep end with those waves pushing us around for a while. We just joked around and acted stupid. Then the water started getting calm, and Jackie said, "I'll be back." And I got out of the pool as he went inside the house. So I just kind of stood there dripping and staring beyond the backyard at all that land, rolling on and on into the night. I got this real satisfied feeling like it was my house, on my ranch, and that huge satellite dish with the stars showing bright over it was mine too.

Just then the pool lights clicked on. Jackie came padding back outside, except he was holding a pitcher and two glasses. He put what he was carrying down on the patio table and went, "You thirsty?"

"Sure," I said, and walked over to where he was busy pouring us drinks.

"Margaritas," he told me, handing me a glass. "I made it this afternoon." Again I thought, "He's okay." And I was amazed about him being only thirteen and knowing how to make a drink like that. "I thought they'd be nice in the evening," he explained, and we were sitting at the patio table by then. The night was really beautiful, all clear and wonderful, and I mentioned to him how much I like the stars. "Me too," he said.

But I don't remember what we talked about after that because we kept drinking those margaritas. But I know we was laughing a lot, like pals and everything. Then he got up, sort of crazy like, with this wild look. Next thing I knew, he'd pulled off his trunks. He stood right in front of me without a thing on, and I saw he'd already got hair down there, though his frame still looked like a kid's. Then he ran along the edge of the pool and—SMACK!— he kind of belly flopped into the water. Then he called to me, "Come on! It's great!"

So I went, "What the hell!" Then I let my trunks fall to my feet, and I stepped out of them and jumped headfirst into the deep end. I mean, I didn't think that much of it because me and Sammy and Lee always skinny-dipped at this watering hole in the Caprock.

Once more me and Jackie got to horsing around. My head spun some from the drinks. I was feeling pretty good. Suddenly we were bouncing off the board together. We were splashing and squirting at each other. Then Jackie swam off by himself. So I hit the board a couple of more times. Then I noticed he was over in the swallow end, sort of doing nothing and being still. He had his chest pressed close against the pool wall. He had his arms folded in front of him on the curb. "What's wrong?" I said, swimming to where he was.

"Nothing," he told me.

I noticed that he was moving himself under the water, real gradual, kind of pushing his hips toward the wall. "What're you doing?"

"Try this."

"What?"

Then he moved from where he was at and went, "Get where I was." So I did. "Put yourself close," he said. And then I felt it. There was a jet of warm air shooting into the pool, hammering against my dick. So immediately I pushed away from the wall because I got scared it was going to hurt. But Jackie was grinning. "Do it again," he said. "I promise. It feels good."

"I don't know."

"Look." He floated his waist up and his dick, all hard and whompyjawed, bobbed for a moment above the water. "It's really good."

And for some reason, I don't know why, my dick got hard just thinking about that jet pushing on it. Next thing I knew, I had myself plastered to that wall, and that warm air vibrated all over my balls and everything. Pretty soon it felt like I might lose my stuff right there in the pool. I knew if it weren't for Jackie being beside me and watching me, his hands between his legs, I'd have gone on and shot already.

"Feels nice, huh?" Jackie said.

"Yeah. It's nice."

"Do this," he said, and then he had his hand on me. He held

my dick and guided it back and forth over the mouth of the jet. I swear, I was so horny that another guy's fingers fiddling with my boner didn't bother me. But my stomach was full of butterflies. Then I got this terrible idea that someone might catch us out there messing around like that.

"We better stop," I said, kicking away from the jet with Jackie's hand still on my dick. "Someone might see."

"Let's go inside, then. My folks won't be home until late."

I don't know why I did it now. I've wondered. But I just don't know. We headed on to Jackie's bedroom, naked as can be. It was his idea to get on the bed, not mine. To be honest, I didn't really know what we was going to do. I was just hard and ready to blow. So then we stretched out side by side, and for a bit we kind of played with ourselves. Then he played with me. And I went, "Don't stop," or, "Faster." Then I shot off like a rocket, sending my junk all across his hand and onto my stomach. And that was all it took for him to cut loose, because he'd been doing me with one hand and himself with the other. His stuff came spurting out, hot and thick, landing on his chest, splashing to the bedding, some of it hitting my arm.

The truth is, once we was finished, I knew we'd screwed up. My whole self just went hollow and sick. It was enough to almost make me want to kill myself. Right away I was saying to Jackie, "We shouldn't have done this. It's wrong what we done." And his face was real pale, like he'd got the same thoughts going on in him. Then I banged my head on the pillow, going, "Stupid! I'm so stupid!" Then Jackie started crying. He was on his back and just sobbing like he was about to die. "This didn't happen," I told him. "How's that? It didn't happen, okay?"

"Okay," he said.

"I won't tell no one, you don't tell no one."

"I won't."

I mean, it was bad enough it happened, bad enough that we was there naked with each other's junk on us, but the worse was how Jackie was, his stomach heaving, his body shaking from tears.

"It's no big deal," I said to him once I'd got myself together some. "It shouldn't have gone on like that, that's all." The sad part was I sort of wished I could've held him then and said, "Don't worry." But to do that wouldn't have been right, especially after what we'd done.

The Duke

Thing I like the most about a shower is how all the dirt on me goes swirling around in the drain, and I'm standing there getting all soapy. I got the heat on until it makes my skin burn red. I about fog the whole bathroom with steam—that way the place don't seem so grungy when I'm done. I sort of give the bathroom a shower too, I guess.

I know there's guys who just hop in and out of the shower. They kind of scrub their pits, maybe once or twice between their legs, then they're finished. Not me. I got a routine, had it since I was twelve, and I stick to it. It's a matter of sixes. Don't ask me why. Six times I go over my legs and arms. Six times on my chest. Six on my neck and face and the bottom of my feet. I even get that soap into the cracks for a sixer, though I don't think it's important that I go on about that. Let's just say that once I'm done, a person could eat a pretty germ-free meal off my body. I mean, nothing like a shower to make a guy feel new.

The worst part of showering is when it's over, because I'm usually so relaxed I don't want to get out. But my skin gets all pruney, and sometimes Mom or Joel's waiting their turn, so I don't stay in as long as I want. The other worst part is when I step into that mess that's our bathroom. No matter how much I bitch and moan, no matter how many times I try and keep it nice, there's always towels hanging on the door or the sink. Mom's got her clothes and stuff all bunched in a corner. There's dark hairs and piss drops on the toilet. And even though Mom says me and Joel do our share, I know that ain't always true. Someone's just got to look at Stump or Bob when they're drunk to know who's doing the share of missing the hole. Anyway, when I get finished peeing, I shake the dew that's left and wipe the seat clean if I leave a drop or two.

My favorite showers are the ones after a game or after I get done working for T.K. Those are the best. I step from that shower feeling about as crisp as a new dollar bill. I stand in front of that smudged mirror, clear away a circle of steam so I can see my face, then I comb my wet hair in about a hundred ways until I get it just perfect. Sometimes I part it to the right, or to the left, depending on how I feel. Then I'm ready to dress for the night, and John Wayne appears on the other side of that circle, he's rumpling his brow at me, saying, "Let's move 'em out, boys! We're burning daylight!"

Soon I'm sparkling fresh in pressed Wranglers with a laundered T-shirt peeking under the collar of my favorite button-up denim shirt. I got on the Polo cologne Hanna gave me for Christmas, and I'm nearly as sharp as one of them guy models in Mom's fashion magazine.

The downer is when I come walking into the living room. Joel's sitting about two feet from the TV. Junie's in the easy chair with a Coors. Joel's already in his pajamas, and Junie's all Mrs. Halter and Scanty Shorts with no shoes on. Her hair ain't been restored since the previous night when Bob took off. She looks a wreck. Her and Joel are watching a videotaped movie called *The Blue Lagoon,* which I remember because that's the first movie I ever saw that actually made me pop a boner, and they're paying no mind to the clutter of beer cans and cigarette butts and plates with dried chunks of food that's all around them.

What gets me about Junie is that she's nothing more than a guest. I mean, her and Bob share this clunk of a trailer in Claude, but she's always out here watching our TV or eating our food or acting like she owns the place. So I say, "Why don't you clean some of this up, Junie." But she ignores me. So I step over and nudge that empty Styrofoam cooler near her feet, and the melted ice water sloshes around inside. "Think you could put this up?"

But again she pays me no mind, except to stick her middle finger in the air without taking her eyes from the TV. So I say, "Boy, you're in a good mood." Then I ask, "Where's Bob," because I know that'll get under her skin real quick.

"I don't know where Bob is and I don't give a damn!" she practically yells, though she keeps her eyes glued to the movie.

So I move right in front of her. She kind of tilts her head to stare past me, takes a sip of her Coors. "Ever quit drinking, Junie?" I say. "Just to see what it's like?"

And that's all it takes. She's got her face squinched at me now. She's sort of waving her arms a bit, making the beer bubble over the mouth of the can. "I'm watching your brother because I told your mama I would," she shouts. "Just don't bug me! It's Saturday night and I'll do what I damn well want to do!" Then she gets all pouty, tilts her head past me again to see the TV, then blows this heavy sigh like she's just made the greatest point ever.

I can't help it. There's just something funny about Junie when she's mad. And old John Wayne thinks it's a hoot too. He's coming out of me, saying to Joel, "Put her to bed, lil' partner, if she has too much," but Joel's too absorbed to hear the Duke.

"Fuck you, William Keeler!" Junie says.

So me and the Duke lean forward and kiss her right on the forehead, which flusters Junie really good. She don't know whether to smile or bomp me on the nose, so she pretends I hadn't laid one on her or nothing. She just flips a hand back and forth at me, like she's shooshing me away or something. "Later—" I tell her. "Hope you have a real fine evening, lil' darlin'," the Duke cuts in. Then me and John are heading for the front door, bending the brim of my Stetson, smelling like a rose, looking like a million, and as I let the screen door slam shut, Junie goes, "I really can't stand you sometimes!"

Lockharts

The only thing I can think to do with old Waylon Lockhart staring down his nose at me is glance around that tidy living room of his. I'm sitting right beside Hanna on the couch, and Waylon's across from us in his big recliner chair. He's dressed like he does at school, which is funny because it's Saturday. He's got on them blue-black slacks, that baby blue short-sleeve shirt with pens and his glasses case in the breast pocket. There's this tall lamp standing beside his chair, lighting up the whole room, casting off that bald head of his.

Sometimes me and Lee joke about how Waylon's got one long strand of hair he wraps around his head so people'll think he's still got something growing there. That always gets me going real good. But I don't think Waylon would see it the same way me and Lee do. He's not what could be called an easygoing fellow. I mean, without a doubt, Waylon's a school principal through and through, even when he's being Hanna's dad.

I don't know how long we've been sitting here with him not saying a word, just studying us, like he's got us all figured out or something. I can't think of anything to say, and Hanna's not helping none. There's this oval clock on the mantel tick tocking, and that's about the only thing making conversation, except for Hanna's mom, who's singing to herself in the kitchen.

Finally Mrs. Lockhart comes walking in with her big smile. She's got these two saucers, each with a helping of peach cobbler and a fork, and she hands them to me and Hanna. Then she perches down on the other side of Hanna and says, "Just baked today, and I knew it'd be a treat for the both of you." So I kind of mumble thanks, because I'm nervous as hell. I pick up that fork and try to eat real slow so I don't seem a pig. And me and Hanna just munch on the cobbler, trying not to pay each other mind, and Mrs. Lockhart and Waylon are watching us eat while that damn clock is saying, "Click clock click clock click clock." And the only other noise is the chewing of my mouth and the tinkling of my fork against the saucer. Then Mrs. Lockhart flashes that big spooky smile and says, "I guess you two are excited about Homecoming."

"Yes, ma'am'," I say around a mouthful of cobbler.

Mrs. Lockhart puts a hand on Hanna's knee and gives her a squeeze as she goes, "Well, it's certainly my favorite time of the school year."

"Yes, ma'am."

Then nothing else. And I'm done eating. Then Waylon leans forward, sort of looks over the top of his glasses, and says to me, "Still haven't decided what you're going to study for yet?"

"No, sir, I guess not."

"Well, son, you better start setting your sails."

And I don't know what to say, but Mrs. Lockhart hops in with, "Willy'll find something he wants when—"

But old Waylon interrupts by waving a hand. "No, no, Ellen," he's saying, "now don't start. I've been a principal at this school for—what is it?—all of fourteen years now. And I can always show you who's going places and who won't. Because if you don't know where you're going, you won't get there. It's as simple as that."

And Mrs. Lockhart is still smiling, but I can tell she's not smiling underneath her face. She says, "Well—"

But Waylon just cuts in again, but this time his tone is a little softer. He's saying to his wife, "We've known Hanna's goal for a long time, haven't we?" Then to Hanna he goes, "Haven't we, baby?" And Hanna forces a big smile, and it's weird because she's suddenly looking just like her mom. But Waylon hardly pays her any attention because he's back to asking Mrs. Lockhart, "Haven't we, Ellen?"

"Well—"

"She's going to Texas Tech and be an educator just like her daddy. Right, baby?" I mean, Hanna's smiling now like her life depends on it or something. Her lips are pushed so far north that I keep waiting for them to pop right off her face. But that don't stop Waylon one bit. He just keeps on rattling, and I'm listening to the whole thing and from the corner of my eyes I can see Mrs. Lockhart's fingers gripping on Hanna's knee harder and harder. "You can have your Dart-mouth or any of the rest of them," he's saying while his wife's knuckles are turning white, "but Tech still puts out the best teachers in the whole country! And it's only a hundred and forty miles from Claude. Yessir, we've known Hanna's goal for a long time now!"

Then it's done with, and we're right back to no talk. Mrs. Lockhart gets up and takes our plates and forks and sort of floats out of the room. And there's that stupid clock yapping away. And for a second I shut my eyes because I can't stand being here. Then all I hear is click clock click clock click clock. And that click clock carries me and Hanna right out of that house into the warm, quiet night.

We're walking along the sidewalk, and there's this distant, low whine of some country song playing from a porch radio somewhere. And Hanna's got her hand in mine, and I got an arm across her shoulders, and she's saying, "Guess I don't get to say much about what I'm going to do. They've always told me I was going to be a teacher."

"Is that what you want to be?"

"I don't know—I guess."

"Your dad don't like me much."

"Yes he does. He's just kind of strange sometimes, you know. I mean, he just worries about me."

Then old Waylon's right there with us, coming out of my

mouth, going, "Well, sir, I've been the principal of this school for—how long is it now?—fourteen years."

Hanna slaps my stomach, saying, "He doesn't sound like that," but she's not mad or nothing.

"He does," I tell her.

"No, he doesn't! I should know."

Then I stop our walking. I slip in behind her. I bring my arms around her waist, pull her close, and whisper in her ear, "He really does."

But she's already onto something else. "You could go to Texas Tech too," she's telling me, sounding excited at the thought. "Coach Bud keeps telling Daddy that you can go to any college you want to, and then we'd be together all the time."

But I don't want to talk no more. I put a finger to her lips, then I take it away all slowly. She kind of snuggles into me. Then I bring my head over her shoulder and kiss her real deep, and there's a part of me that's hoping that old Waylon is somewhere nearby, that he's hiding behind a tree or bush and watching me put my tongue in his daughter's mouth.

Homecoming

The whole darn town and the whole darn school and just about everyone in the county gets all worked up for that night when me and the team burn that huge stack of wood, old lumber scraps, just about anything we can get our hands on, for the homecoming pep rally bonfire at the practice field. Everyone parks their cars and trucks in sort of a circle around the blazing wood, except they do it before the wood is torched.

Now all the townfolks and teachers and students, and a bunch of folks I ain't never seen before, stand behind the team and Coach Bud and Coach Slick as we sort of huddle near that big chunk of oily-smelling lumber—oily because Mr. Coupland, our History teacher and FFA supervisor, spent the afternoon putting some nasty kind of tar-like crap here and there on the bonfire so it'd take off even if some kid were just to aim a magnifying glass at it the wrong way. He went a little overboard with the stuff, if truth be known, and Coach Bud said to me after practice, "Careful you don't go and burn your eyebrows, son." He told me that because this year I get to toss the torch into the mess. That's because I'm the captain and I'm a senior. Last year Andrew Granite got the honor, and now he's standing in the crowd with his letter jacket on gazing right at me as Coach Bud puts that torch in my hand. And old Andrew's wearing this real serious expression, like he don't care one way or the other that he's no longer part of the team, but I know he wishes he were back in time with us. Maybe that's why I always hear him yelling like nuts from the stands during games. Maybe that's why a lot of the guys who graduated last year come to the games drunk and cheer louder than almost anybody else for the Tigers.

It's kind of sad to see a guy like Andrew because he wasn't much of a player to begin with and he ain't that smart and now he works for the highway department filling potholes on 287. I never much liked him anyway, cocky son of a bitch, but I give him a little nod so he'll know I'm thinking about him before I put that torch in the pile. The thing is he don't like me much either, so he acts all cool like he don't even know I'm around. He don't like me for all sorts of reasons, but mostly because I'm a better player than he was, because Hanna's my girl and not his. I mean, he'd asked her to go with him to the sports banquet when he was a senior, he sent her flowers and everything, but she had to tell him she was going with me. I felt kind of bad when he came alone to the banquet, but what was I supposed to do?

All the same, I'm sure he started hating me during his senior year when me and Lee ribbed him pretty hard because he wore all his UIL medals on his letter jacket one day like he was a general or something. He walked around the halls with those stupid things hanging on his tit for nearly a week, until Lee and I just couldn't let it go on. We thought we was doing him a favor by saluting when he came into class, calling him Sergeant Knownothing or Captain Bullshit, kind of trying to give him a clue on what everyone in school was thinking. I mean, Jesus, even the teachers thought he looked silly.

But Andrew didn't take our kidding too well. He caught Lee going to his pickup one afternoon and took a swing at him, nailing Haywood right on the forehead, leaving this big red circle where his senior ring smushed into the space between Lee's eyes. Then he threw Lee to the pavement and said, "If you and your boyfriend don't shut up I'll kill you!" Imagine that. Like I said, he ain't that bright. Needless to say, once Coach Bud sat him down and explained that them medals were for bedroom shelves or for his mother to frame, Andrew finally figured it out. The funny thing is that red spot on Lee's forehead where Andrew sucker-punched him stayed there for about a week, so me and Sammy had a royal time laying into him, calling him Gandhi or Gunga Din, but at least Lee can have a laugh at himself.

Anyway, the whole crowd is carrying on like there's no tomorrow. Hanna and the rest of the cheerleaders are over to one side with the pep squad, and they're doing the "Let it burn, Let it burn, Let it burn" hurrah, kicking their legs, clapping their hands, which has got the herd all excited.

Everyone's watching me, so I just wave that torch over my head. I wave it this way, and everyone goes, "Burn it!" Then I wave it over here, and they all go, "Let it burn!" So I turn around and give that torch one good flip through the air, and it goes spinning like a firecracker into the middle of that stinky pile. WHOOSH! And Mr. Coupland's mix explodes, and that fire blazes up without a hitch.

Right away the heat shoots at me. My face gets all warm and dry. My neck gets hot. I don't know how long I'm standing at the edge of the bonfire, but pretty soon everyone gets all quiet. I don't hear nothing except the wood splintering and hissing. I hardly notice that the team has stepped back. But I can't take my eyes from the flames as they leap higher and almost seem to dance. I'm staring at this creaky wreck of an outhouse that me and Lee and Sammy found to put on top of the pile, and just the sight of the thing, with all the paint and stuff we splashed on it, gets me all happy inside. And it's kind of peaceful being by the bonfire, sort of comforting and safe.

Before I know it, Coach Slick is yanking me backwards. He pulls me close, puts an arm on my shoulder, and I see these eerie orange and black shadows move over his face. Then I glance around at the team and Coach Bud, and they're all gazing with these blank expressions, like they're somewhere deep inside that firey, crackling stack. So I give a glance at the crowd and see they're lost and far away like the team. Suddenly I get a creepy thought from *Night of the Living Dead*, when them zombies are going across the front yard toward that house where them people are holed up. So I turn around real quick. And for a moment I imagine that I'm the only living person in Claude. I start thinking of Andrew coming at me from behind, his arms sticking out, moving all clumsy to take a bite from my head, which is pretty dumb really. And I think if it weren't for that outhouse, I'd probably be a bit more spooked now.

It was Sammy's idea to steal the outhouse. We seniors had already collected all the wood that was needed for the bonfire, and me and Lee and Sammy were on our way to meet Stump and Bob after practice. There we were in Lee's pickup. We had the radio playing something by Willie Nelson, but I don't know what because I don't like Willie Nelson that much. We're just speeding along this nowhere stretch of dirt road outside of town, going to where Stump told us to go, and Sammy started screaming, "Go back! Go back!" And me and Lee didn't know what he was going on about, but by his face we knew it was important. But instead of turning the truck around, Lee threw the thing in reverse and drove us rear end first into the same dust his truck had just spit up. He was going nearly fifty with a wild grin and I went, "Goddamn, Lee," because all I saw was dirt coming at us.

And then Sammy shouted, "Slow down! Stop! Stop!" So Lee hit the brakes and a ton of junk from his dashboard came flying at us—notebooks, a couple of pens, a Skoal can, work gloves.

For a moment we sort of sat there waiting for the dust to clear from the road. The whole time Sammy was gazing out the window. Then all slowly that outhouse came into view on the other side of this barbed-wire fence, and Sammy was pointing at it, looking to us, then back at it, still pointing. Then Lee said, "Hell, Sammy, if you had to take a dump why didn't you say so?"

I'd have given a million bucks for a photograph of Stump's face when we pulled in next to his pickup with that gray, peeling, rickety shitter in the bed of Lee's truck. There was Stump with his sunglasses on, trying to be his usual laid-back self with one arm hanging over the driver's door, but once he caught sight of that outhouse, his lips sort of parted, his arm drew on into the truck to remove them sunglasses. We jumped from Lee's pickup, all dirty from having just spent twenty minutes removing and carrying a true treasure of the West Texas Historical Preservation Society from private property, and Stump didn't know whether to laugh or start his pickup to get away for us. "I don't even want to know," he finally said, shaking his head like we're insane or something, which got me and Sammy and Lee bursting out real hard.

Once we settled down some, I started in with, "You got them?" I was practically climbing through the driver's window of Stump's pickup. Sammy and Lee were pushing in behind me, like crazed ferrets or something.

"Course I did," Stump said, and he grinned at Bob, who was sitting across from him in the truck. I noticed Bob was holding a grocery sack in his lap.

"Hey, thanks, Stump!"

"Yeah, yeah."

"Grew up with an outhouse like that," Bob said, handing the rumpled brown sack to Stump, who handed it out the window to me.

Lee went and dipped his arm into the bag, brought out a fifth of Old Crow. And Sammy got his arm in there too, fishing around until he found the box of Trojans. "Yeah, man, one size fits all," Sammy said, "except Sammy!"

And Lee went, "Yeah, they're too big for you," which was so stupid I had to smile.

"Not a word about where you got this," Stump told me, then glanced around like someone might be lurking, even though we're in the middle of the Caprock, down this thin cattle trail where the only lurkers are flies on cow dung.

"Don't worry," I said.

"Hey, you opened our rubbers," Lee said to Stump. He had the Trojans box now, aiming a finger at where the cardboard top had been torn.

Bob leaned over Stump. He had that ugly rotten-teeth grin. "That's what you call sharing the goods, son," he cackled.

"Hell, the whole team couldn't use a box of rubbers with a road map," Stump said, grinning at Bob like he'd said the cleverest thing on the planet. But before we could dispute the whereabouts of the rest of them Trojans, Stump went, "Just be careful who sees that bottle. I could get my ass in a real crack!"

"No one's going to know," I told him.

"Better not," he said, cranking the truck, "or else I'll have to report that crapper there in the truck." Then, as he shifted the gear stick, he went, "Just get me a twenty-point spread, all right?"

"You got it," Sammy said.

Stump gave us a little flick of his wrist, then him and Bob went bouncing off, the pickup churning dust as it glided away on the dirt road.

So as Sammy divided the rubbers between us, Lee twisted the cap from the Old Crow. I put my nose over the bottle and took a whiff, which about knocked me on my ass. "Not bad," Lee said.

"Pretty bad," I told him.

Then the three of us spent the better part of yesterday night in Lee's garage with that outhouse and the Old Crow. We got all silly and stuff, sort of hammered, as we went about decorating that thing with green and gold paint, which is the colors of the Guthrie Jaguars, who also happen to be our homecoming rivals. I wrote BUST THE JAGUARS in yellow on the whompyjawed door, and Sammy put TIGER POWER ALL THE WAY on one side, but Lee made him paint over it with green because he didn't like the idea of our team's name getting eaten by flames.

I don't know who got the idea of the dummy, but I think it was Lee. Like I said, we was pretty gone. Anyway, we filled some ratty old Wranglers and a T-shirt with newspaper. We made the pants green and the shirt yellow, because we wanted everyone to get the notion that they was looking at an official Guthrie Jaguar. I mean, we were in total hysterics by the time we set that dummy on the toilet seat. Sammy stuck a mop down the shirt and into the pants so it sat upright and looked like it had a head, and we kept going on and on about how great it'd be to catch one of them Guthrie boys on a toilet like this. How funny and strange it'd be for that boy to open the door and see that he was on top of the bonfire and about to be burnt before the cheering people of Claude.

We were three drunk and happy outhouse robbers. I don't know how long we just stood around in that garage admiring our work with all its green and yellow splashes and words here and there. "We're the only people in the universe," Lee said, which seemed to make a lot of sense then.

"That's right," Sammy said. "We are."

Then Lee gave that outhouse a little kiss on the crescent moon that had been carved on the door. So I gave it a kiss too. And Sammy took the last swig of Old Crow before pressing his lips to the moon.

By the time we brought that outhouse and toilet to the bonfire pile, we'd lost Lee. It was almost midnight and we were really drunk. Lee'd helped me and Sammy load the mess into his truck, then he ambled off and vomited Old Crow and pizza and whatever else was in him in the bushes under his folks' bedroom window. Next thing me and Sammy knew, he was facedown on the lawn, sort of kicking his legs on the grass, sort of flapping his arms like he was about to fly away or something. I had to dig around in his pants pocket to get his truck keys, then we told him we'd be back and headed on without him.

To be honest, I don't remember much after that. I don't know how me and Sammy climbed that mountain of wood to set that outhouse on top. I just don't know. But somehow we did it, and the next morning it was there for everyone to see. One problem was we couldn't get it to stand, so the outhouse with the dummy inside had to be laid on its side. The other problem was that we rested it with the flimsy door pressing shut against the pile, so no one could know there was a Guthrie dummy boy waiting to be surprised.

So now I'm watching the whole thing burn, watching the out-house pop and bend with flames, and I can't help but imagine that stupid dummy all wilting and consumed inside. For some reason I feel sort of sorry for him, like I wish we hadn't put him there. Maybe he's like a voodoo doll or something. Maybe right now in Guthrie there's some kid rolling around and screaming and everybody don't got any notion of what to do about it. I know it sounds kind of stupid, but I just wish we'd left those Wranglers and that T-shirt and that mop alone.

"How you feeling?" Coach Slick whispers.

"Fine," I say, and he gives my shoulder a little squeeze with his hand.

I guess he asked me that because he can tell from my face that I ain't acting all churchful like the rest of the team or the town, what with me frowning at the sight of that old outhouse breaking apart. Or he might have asked because I got sick after practice, on account of Coach Bud made me and Lee and Sammy and Harvey run an extra mile this afternoon. I had a real rotten hangover most of the day and I guess the running did me in. I got back to the locker room and nearly passed out. Then when I was showering with Lee and Sammy nearby, I got these pains in my side and—BLAM!—there shot my lunch, all chunky and pink, pouring out of me to the tile floor. I mean, Lee and Sammy flew from the showers like they was being chased by bulls or something, except they was cracking jokes and acting all grossed. Next thing I know, Coach Slick was standing over me turning off the water. I was bent over the drain, thinking I might konk over in my own crud. Then he was kind of patting my back, saying, "Get it all out," which I know was meant in a nice way, so I didn't tell him I'd already gotten it all out. "Coach put too much on you today, huh?" he said. "Can I get you anything?"

"I don't think so, Slick," I told him, my head twirling around so fast I had to shut my eyes. Then I realized I'd called him Slick, which was something we almost never said to his face. It's not that he minds being called that, it's just that it don't seem right saying it to him. I mean, Lee gave Coach Mangum the nickname of Slick because that's how his hair is, all slicked back with gel and perfect. It don't matter what's going on—if he's been running with us or shouting from the sidelines, his hair just sits on his head unmoved. Anyway, he didn't seem to notice or nothing that I'd called him that.

The thing about Slick is that he ain't that old, maybe in his twenties, I ain't sure, but he's a great guy to just hang out with. Because he's only the assistant football coach he don't say much, except to echo something from Coach Bud, but he's a lot easier than Coach Bud to just sit around with after practice or a game and chew the fat. I think it's because he's not much older than the rest of us. I know me and Sammy and Lee, we sort of admire him because he was a wide receiver Oklahoma State Cowboy, and because he don't talk to us like we're kids. In a way, he's just one of us, except he gets paid to act like a coach or something.

Before practice this afternoon, before I got sick and everything, Slick was standing in the doorway of Coach Bud's office combing his hair as if it weren't already fine. I was at the lockers with Sammy and Lee and big old Harvey, and we were still getting our practice gear on, even though the rest of the team was already suited and on the floor near Slick's feet. Then Slick went, "All right! You all settle down and listen up," because everyone was horsing around and talking like we do. And it got all quiet. All of us stopped and stared at Slick, who was putting his comb away and saying, "Pay attention to this, okay?" And he had a deadly serious face on, which he always gets in the locker room before practice. "Miss Walt complained again to Mr. Lockhart about the profanity during practice, so you guys watch it, okay?" Then someone was grumbling by Slick's feet, and someone else was kind of laughing, and Slick aimed his finger at whoever it was and went, "All right, just watch it." And there were some mumbles of "Okay" and "No problem, Coach."

Then Coach Bud came out of his office. He sort of stepped in next to Slick, and I knew it was time to just stop what I was doing and listen. So did the other guys. It don't matter if we're not all dressed or sitting on the floor like we're supposed to, Coach Bud expects us to freeze and pay him attention. "Okay, boys, half-speed today," he said in a casual, offhand way, which made me happy because I knew it'd be a light practice and I was still feeling crappy from the Old Crow. "We'll go over a few changes for the defense—won't show them anything new on the offense. We'll just keep sticking it in their ear, maybe throw a little to Earl or Izzy to keep them honest. They'll key Willy with the middle backer, and Harvey'll tend to him. Jesse'll pick up any blitzing, which I don't think'll amount to much. If they want to zone us, fine. Sammy'll take them right downtown. I want a good first quarter. That's the main thing, okay? I don't want anybody back on their heels until we've got them good and licked. Understand?" Then Coach Bud squinted his eyes around at us, crossed his arms, and we all sort of nodded our heads and stuff so he'd know we were following him.

For a moment, Coach Bud seemed kind of deep in his own thoughts, like he wasn't quite sure on what he was about to say. His brow got all wrinkled. He glanced at Slick, then he shook his head a bit. So Slick shook his head some too. Then Coach Bud squatted to look right at the faces of those guys on the floor and said, "I don't like Saturday games because it takes us out of our rhythm, but we can't help it." He was saying this very seriously, like he was telling us some private secret or something. He was still shaking his head, going, "This Homecoming's a pain in the ass, but it's something we got to live with, so we'll do it. After they burn that big pile of crap tonight, don't horse around too long. Get rest and be ready to suit up at five on Saturday. Got it?" So all of us nodded again and some of us even mumbled "Right" or "Sure."

Coach Bud stood upright. He pulled his shoulder blades in, which I remember being called scapulas in Anatomy. His back popped some, then he went, "All right, let's get on over to the field, and no jackassing around!" And the guys on the floor jumped to their feet, their cleats clacking, and started heading out of the locker room with Slick leading the way.

Us at the lockers were going real fast trying to finish dressing, and Coach Bud was staring right at us now. He was tilting his head to one side. I could see him from the corner of my eyes. "We're busted," I heard Sammy whisper.

Lee was fumbling with his laces. Harvey was pulling on his pads. Sammy was already done. I still had my cleats left to do.

"You boys back there," said Coach Bud. "I want you to stay after practice." And my stomach sank because I knew we were in for it. "You seem to enjoy taking your time here, so I got a little extra running for you. You all look like you could use a little extra running, don't you think?"

"Okay," I told him, my scapulas slumping.

"Sure," Lee and Sammy said disgusted, giving each other quick pissed glances.

"No problem," Harvey grumbled. Then under his breath he went, "Pig," which made me want to burst out, though I had to hold it in, because Coach Bud had his brow wrinkled again, his arms crossed, his left foot sort of tap tap tapping on the locker room tile.

The thing is, I thought I'd be all right doing the running. I thought that I might be able to jog off that hangover. Boy, was I wrong about that. I mean, before I lost it in the showers, my stomach was hurting something awful, all sharp and twisty, as my cleats was bang banging around the practice field. Then once I'd blown my lunch, I felt a lot better, but my knees were all wobbly and I was pale and weak. I must've been a sad sight, because Coach Slick had to help me to my feet in the shower. Then he got me a towel and had me sit down in Coach Bud's office and take these huge breaths. I guess I'm lucky that Coach Bud wasn't around, otherwise he might have given me some real shit for getting sick before the Saturday game.

•   •   •

I guess for a lot of folks the high point of the bonfire is when we sing the school song. The pep squad and cheerleaders get it going. Those girls just open their mouths and out it comes, real low at first, until it spreads to the team and then to the people in the crowd. Suddenly we're all doing it. We're all going, "Cheer, cheer for Claude High School's fame," except those words aren't coming from my mouth. I'm just moving my lips because I think the song is sort of corny, and I feel dumb when I sing anyway. But I'm about the only one in the county who feels like that.

Everyone else, from the littlest of kids to old men and farmers and women in these print dresses and cowboys, they got no problem with chirping, "Bring down the echoes shouting its name, send a hearty cheer on high, shake down the thunder from the sky!" Or, "But though the odds be great or small, Claude High School Tigers win over all, while her loyal sons go marching!" But not me. No way. Only a housewife could come up with words like that. The whole thing makes me think of those poems Hanna writes on the back of napkins at the Dairy Mart. Things like, "Our love makes waves," and, "He dreams of rainbow catches, she wills it so." Stuff like that.

What really gets me is that the singing sounds awful. There ain't a soul in tune. Those voices are all over the place. I mean, the crunch and rustle of the fire is a billion times more nice to listen to. It's enough to get me and Lee and Sammy cracking jokes, except there they are, all intense and stuff, singing that song like they're praying or something.

And even though I'm supposed to be serious at this moment, sort of letting them words come from my heart to my lips, I can't help but glance over my shoulder at the crowd. And dammit if I don't lock eyes with Andrew Granite, who I swear is giving me the nastiest squint I've ever seen in my life. And he ain't singing at all. He's just giving me that look that says, "I hate you." It's almost as if he wants to come charging forward and knock me into them flames.

So I blow him a kiss. I don't know why. I just do it. I figure it'll ruffle him good. I pucker my lips and send him a good one, all sneaky, right under everyone else's noses. And I'll be damn, that stupid bastard goes and shoots a kiss right back at me. Then he shrugs some like I ain't worth nothing. Then he just turns around and pushes through the crowd, leaving me a bit rattled.

So I stick a hand in one of my tail pockets so I'll seem casual and everything, like I can fool myself to thinking that Andrew didn't best me or anything. I glance to the bonfire and notice that our outhouse is a big hunk of orange cinders. And as Coach Slick takes his arm from my shoulder, my fingers press against the two Trojans I got saved by my wallet, and just then the school song ends and the crowd cheers, "Onward to Vic-to-reeee!"

Nebraska

I got Bruce Springsteen with just his guitar and harmonica on my tape deck, going, "Me and her went for a ride, sir, and ten innocent people died," which gives me a good case of the chills each time he goes and sings that. It's the same tape I play over and over again these days when I'm in the mood to get all lonesome and thoughtful, even if I ain't particularly thoughtful about nothing at the moment, even if I ain't too lonesome either because I got Hanna in the cab of my truck and we're almost stretched across the seat in each other's arms.

We're parked in our usual spot, that hidden little mesquite pasture, except tonight we got company. Sammy and his girl Lilah, who's about the most beautiful black girl I've ever seen, are getting comfortable on a blanket in the bed of my truck, and Lee's parked nearby with Hanna's best friend Patricia, who also happens to be Lee's girlfriend. Then there's big ol' Harvey and skinny ol' Liz messing around in the backseat of Harvey's coppertone Buick Riviera with white sidewalls. It's really his dad's car, something special that Harvey Sr. sometimes lets his son drive around town on Friday nights, but Harvey says it'll be his by graduation.

"Can you put the radio on?" Hanna says. "I'm getting depressed."

"No," I say, and give her a little smooch on the forehead.

I guess I can't blame her. To be honest, I thought Bruce Spingsteen was supposed to be a little more rocking than this, a little more happy and loud. In fact, the only reason I bought the damn tape was because it was called *Nebraska*, which is where I've always dreamed of playing college ball. I swear to God, that's why I laid out ten bucks for it. Nebraska. Sort of like a sign or something. I mean, I nearly returned that tape because it was so down and out sad to listen to, like hearing a coyote howl or a train whistle or thunder rumble in the Caprock. I remember wondering on how many Bruce Springsteens there were, because this sure as hell wasn't the fellow who's always singing about glory days and all that. But I was wrong, and sure enough them songs grew on me until I can't imagine not ever liking them in the first place.

"Goddammit," I say when Hanna goes and turns the tape player off.

"Don't do that to the Lord," she tells me. "Let's just have some quiet, Willy," which would normally be fine with me, but the thing is there ain't no quiet where we are tonight. Most times there's just the wind or crickets or the shocks on the truck squeaking or stuff like that. But now we got Harvey and Liz making a racket in the Buick. And even though we should roll up the windows, me and Hanna can't help but pay them some attention.

"Harvey," Liz is about shouting, "you're smashing me!"

"It's okay—" Harvey tells her.

"It ain't okay! I can't breathe!"

"It's okay—"

Then they get all quiet, and Hanna whispers, "Can you imagine?"

"I guess," I say, though I ain't sure what it is I'm supposed to imagine.

Then Hanna starts nibbling on my earlobe, which she knows drives me out of the world. Then she stops all abruptly because now it's Lee and Patricia's turn to cause a ruckus for everyone to hear, and I can't help but wish Bruce was singing something so I wouldn't have them others taking Hanna's mind from me.

"Hanna—" I kind of sigh in a way so she'll get the idea that I don't care one bit about Lee and Patricia.

"Shut up," she whispers, and that about riles me something awful.

Then I hear them, all muffled and distant, and there's Patricia going, "No, Lee, I don't care if you've got one. It might have a hole in it."

And Lee goes, "It don't."

And now me and Hanna are sort of laughing to ourselves as Patricia says, "But what if it does?"

And when Lee says, "Dammit, it's a new one," I know he'd be right pissed if he had any notion that we was hearing his business. I mean, Jesus, when he goes, "New ones don't have holes in 'em," me and Hanna are grinding our heads into each other's shoulders and trying not to burst out.

Then the truck shakes some, and Sammy yells from the bed, "Lee, will you guys keep it down over there!" And that seems to do the trick, because suddenly it's almost like no one else is out here except me and Hanna. There's the soft blowing of the cold breeze coming in the windows, some crickets harping, and I can pretend that the Garth Brooks song coming from Harvey's car is on my radio.

I get my tongue in Hanna's mouth, and she's kind of squeezing my ass with one hand, sort of digging her nails into my Wranglers to where it almost hurts. Then I'm right on top of her. I'm sort of giving her these short thrusts between her legs. And she's breathing real heavy like me. I know she can feel it there through her clothes, all hard and everything, just going back and forth. And I'm thinking about them Trojans in my pocket. I'm wanting her to slip one on me. Then I'm wanting her to unzip my pants and put her mouth down there, and the thought of that gets some junk coming out of me in a hurry, making my shorts all sticky and stuff. And just when I'm about to undo her shirt so I can get my fingers under her bra, she pushes me away, saying, "I got to go!"

But I ain't ready to stop. I'm all sweaty and breathing fast, asking, "A little while?"

She shakes her head, though I can tell she don't want to leave.

Then she stares at me for a long time, as if she don't know what to do. "I can't, Willy," she finally says. "Tomorrow night I get an extra hour for the dance—"

So I slide over behind the wheel, kind of mumbling, "A whole extra hour—" And she can see I'm sort of tense now and irritated, so she sits up and cuddles against me.

"I love you," she says, "you know that. But I got to get home."

The thing is, I can't get that mad at her. If she had her way we'd have just gone on and spent the whole night parked here. But, man, if she's something like a minute late home, that Mr. Lockhart would be on the horn to Sheriff Branches or someone. He'd have a search squad combing the streets. He'd be waiting for me at my house. So I just relax and put my arm around her. "Okay," I sigh, "I know."

Then Hanna goes, "Just think. Someday, when we're married, it'll just be us and no one else. It'll just be us to do what we want to do anytime we want to. Do you think of that?"

"Yeah," I say, even though I ain't really ever thought that much on it.

Hanna gives me this tight hug. Then she says, "We got to go—"

So I shout out the driver's window to Sammy and Lilah, "Hang on! We're going!"

"No, man, not yet," I hear Sammy say, but I already got the engine cranked.

"We're rolling!" I yell, and Sammy goes, "Aw, man!" And when I swerve the truck from the trees and onto the dirt road, the taillights shine red and I catch Sammy and Lilah in my rearview, bundling together in a wool blanket. And they got that blanket wrapped around them like a poncho or something.

"It's getting cold," Hanna says, snuggling herself so close that I can feel a boob against my ribs.

"Yeah," I say, putting the tape player on, letting Bruce come on into the cab. And I turn him up a little louder than usual because I know Hanna ain't going to say nothing about it now. And when he goes, "Sheriff, when the man pulls that switch, sir, and snaps my poor head back, you make sure my pretty baby is sittin' right there on my lap," I can't help but wish it's me and Hanna he's singing about.

Slick's Offering

That's where we find ourselves when we ain't getting none or after we've got some—Whitey Fontane's Exxon station. It don't matter that it's almost midnight and cool outside and the station is closed. At least the Coke machine is stocked, and there's this decent view of Main Street, except now it's all dark and deserted and there ain't nothing to see but nothing.

Me and Sammy was the first ones here after having gone and dropped Hanna and Lilah off. I pulled my truck along the side of the station, then me and Sammy got Cokes. Then we opened the tailgate and just sat there waiting, kind of talking about our girls, and Sammy says how he someday plans to build a little ranch somewhere for him and Lilah to live on. And I got my eyes halfway on the stars and the street lamps of Claude, kind of imagining what it'd be like to have a place like Sammy's talking about.

Then pretty soon Lee comes chugging up sniffing his fingers for us to see, like he's trying to tell us where they've been. Then that handsome Buick with Harvey and his bigass grin appear. And it ain't long before Coach Slick is here too, and he's got Jackie Maitland with him on account of he sometimes has one or two of the younger guys spend the weekend over at his place for videos and poker and things like that. He can get away with it because, like I said, he ain't that old and don't got a wife or a sweetheart to bug him. These days, him and Jackie are on this photography kick. They plan these Saturday morning trips out into the Caprock. They got their maps and cameras and stuff. Go figure.

Before the sun hits the sky, they're climbing between barbed wire and taking pictures of all sorts of stuff—empty farmhouses and dead things, like bloated cows and wild pigs all crappy with maggots, and nature shots of these barrel cactuses sprouting little flowers. Some of it's pretty good, like these ones Coach Slick got of Jackie standing high on a windmill ladder, and Jackie don't got a shirt on, and the moon is still in the sky, and there's all these horses drinking from the trough below. I like that one a lot, though I don't know why they don't take those pictures in color. I guess it's because Jackie's the annual staff photographer and all the shots he does is in black and white. I just think color is better. I don't know why.

Anyway, the bunch of us is either sitting on my tailgate or leaning against the back bumper of the Buick. We got our Cokes and Sprites or whatever, and Coach Slick is telling us his story again, the one he always tells when we ask him to. And even though we've all heard it maybe a dozen times, we're just as interested like it's brand new to our ears. And I know Coach Slick don't mind spinning it once more, because his voice gets all fast and his eyes, I swear, sort of sparkle like he's imagining something we can't even fix in our heads. He's kind of waving his hands above us, saying, "And then you come out of the tunnel right out into the Astrodome—huge, like the fucking galaxy—and the crowd goes all the way up to the sky—and they're all yelling and screaming—and then—right then—all these butterflies in my stomach turn into bucking horses—and I can't believe it, because for weeks all I could think about was playing in that Bluebonnet Bowl, playing against the Razorbacks—on national TV—and then I'm out on the field—all I can think is—I'm about to throw up!"

He takes this heavy breath, slowing his tone some, and goes, "I'm finally there and I'm thinking—I'm about to throw up in front of sixty thousand people—and maybe a million more on TV! And I'm praying—dear God—please—please—I don't want to be the only Oklahoma State Cowboy to ever lose it at the Bluebonnet Bowl!"

And I think we'd all be laughing at the thought of that if it weren't for Coach Slick's face at the moment, which is so confused looking and, well, in the dumps. Like in a flash he's gone from all cheerful to stuck alone on an island or something. He ain't saying a word now, just sort of gazing at that black hole beyond Main Street. And even though I know how his story ends, I go ahead and ask, "So what happened, Coach?"

Then Slick smiles from one corner of his mouth, sighs a bit, and almost whispers, "What happened was, I went and caught three passes for thirty-eight yards. Not much. But I wouldn't trade that one night for all the Christmas presents in the world. Not for all the fur in Dallas."

"You nearly made the pros, didn't you?" Harvey says, but in a quiet, respectful way.

"Nah, not really," Coach Slick says. "Dogging every training camp west of the Mississippi ain't what you'd call nearly making the pros. I tell you, boys, when you get up there to the pros, all that's left is the fastest, meanest, nastiest ones of all, and it didn't take 'em long to lose me." And even though he's talking to us all, he puts his stare right on me and goes, "That's why I still hurt a little every time I see you boys suit up. I'm telling you there ain't a feeling as god-awful lonesome as knowing you're never going to put on them pads again, as knowing it's finally over."

And then he just stops. And none of us has a notion of what to say or do because the story finished all different this time around. And suddenly me and the others got our heads bent toward our feet, we're toying with the tops of our Cokes or scraping our boots against the asphalt, and, with that big Exxon sign humming above us, I know there ain't much more to be said tonight.

Ramona with the Black Eye

I should be asleep right now. I should've been asleep hours ago, what with the big Homecoming game tomorrow. But I can't get her out of my head, so she's to blame, I guess. When I came through the living room door, I almost expected to find Mom and the others already trashed with a case of the Friday night hooplas, except I'd forgotten Mom was doing her catering or banquet thing that she does and Bob and Stump had gone on a deer hunt with this fellow they kept calling Mr. Highhand and Double Aces. It'd even slipped by me that Joel was at Chubby's for the night.

So there I was coming into a dark house with everything all still and quiet inside. And the TV was on, some movie with that punch-happy guy who married Madonna, but the sound wasn't playing from it at all. Junie had herself on the couch with her legs sort of pulled to her chest, and she gave me a concerned glance as I shut the door. I mean, I'd already walked a few steps before I realized someone else was there too.

She was sitting across from Junie in the big stuffed chair, smoking a cigarette, so at first I thought it was Mom already home from work. When I clicked on the lamp by the couch, Junie went, "God, Willy, we wanted it off," and I was about to tell Junie, "Tough shit," but I'd already noticed that it wasn't Mom or anyone else I knew resting in that chair.

The sight of her kind of stopped any words from popping out of me because her lips were so puffy and black-blue, one of her eyes was the same way. She had these nasty welts around her chin, like someone had laid into her with a hammer or something. And that wasn't all. I mean, even though she appeared a mess—

imagine some gal who'd just tried to kiss the grill of a speeding diesel truck—I couldn't help but stare at her for all the wrong reasons. It was like without that swollen and bruised skin, that banged eye, I knew she was a knockout. Never mind that she was at least as old as Mom or as skinny as some bird dog. And when I spotted them tears kind of sliding along her cheeks to that wrecked mouth, I almost wanted to cry for her.

"This is Ramona," Junie said to me, but she said it in this hushed voice. Then she told Ramona, "This is Pug's other boy." But Ramona was somewhere else. She didn't pay me any attention or nothing, just smoked that cigarette and cried without a noise, keeping her eyes on a pair of redder-than-red pumps by her naked feet. So Junie shook her head slow and sad, saying, "Ramona's had kind of a rough night, Willy."

Jesus, I didn't know what to say, so I just shrugged. I didn't do it in a mean way or nothing, but I guess it could've seemed like that. Really, I wanted so badly to say something to make Ramona smile or feel better, but instead I turned around with the thought of climbing into bed.

"Willy?" Junie was saying in her sweet voice. Then suddenly I'd done nearly a whole circle and was standing at the couch again, kind of rubbing my aching eyes with two fingers, Three Stooges style, as Junie gently patted my pants leg and went, "Hon, could you run her back over to Amarillo? Your mama's gone in the car and—"

"Sure," I said, and almost wanted to smack myself because my mouth had moved quicker than my brain.

We was halfway to Amarillo before that Ramona even spoke. There I was on U.S. 287 trying to stay awake by listening to a tape Stump had given me, some songs by this guy Roy Orbison, who sounds pretty good in the middle of the night, singing, "Only the lonely," or, "In dreams I walk with you." And Ramona had herself slumped against the passenger's door, just pushed into the blackness there like a wadded bunch of laundry, like some big raggedy doll. I thought she'd konked out because from the time the truck turned onto the highway she didn't move or nothing.

Forever it seemed I was driving by myself, just gazing at where the headlights lit the road ahead, half paying attention to the music, half thinking about how good it'd be once I got home and flopped down on my bed, when I heard her say, "It's nice of you to do this."

"It's no problem," I said.

Then she leaned forward from that darkness, smoothing the rumples along the lap of that green and purple jack-in-the-pulpit dress of hers. "I've known Pug for a long time," she said. "She's a good person."

"Yeah."

"She gave me a ride, said I could stay at your house until—" She kind of breathed deeply and then said in this wispy, tired way, "I figure I might as well just go back—"

And then she was running her fingers through her hair, kind of making it right again, and I caught a whiff of her perfume, which smelled like ice cream, like vanilla or something sweet like that.

Before long we was leaving I-40 and cruising in this creepy downtown area of Amarillo. Ramona was saying, "Turn left here," and, "Go right at the next light." And there didn't seem to be another car or truck moving on them streets, no folks on them dim sidewalks, just these ratty old buildings, and I got that spooky idea like it was only me and her and Amarillo and the Panhandle and no one else, which felt about as hollow as them buildings we was passing, about as empty as some paper sack or beer can getting flattened under my tires.

Next thing I knew, I was pulling against the curb in front of the Royal Hotel, which didn't look so hot—four floors of dirty-red brick with a bar called Roughnecks, all tinted windows and bright Coors neon, sitting right besides the lobby doors. Right away I saw an older businessman guy almost jogging from the hotel. He seemed sort of hurried, even a little worried, like he was trying to get the hell out of there. He had his hands dancing around his suit coat, patting here and there, as if he might have lost something. He was so wrapped up in what he was doing that he nearly walked straight into this Bouffant Woman, who was heading into the Royal and who obviously had a thing for leather. I mean, leather skirt and jacket, leather boots. It was like if that skirt had gone any higher it would've been a belt. If those boots had been any higher they'd have been pants. If that poofed hair had been any higher it'd have been a monument. So she sort of said something to the businessman guy, something nasty I figured, because he got all goofy, head down and everything, and practically took off running along the sidewalk.

"You live here?" I said to Ramona, who was checking herself in my rearview, who was dabbing pink stuff on her bruises from this small cosmetic case she'd kept in her purse, and was smacking her lips from the lipstick she'd just put on.

"I guess I do," she said, and suddenly her face had a scanty, bitter expression. Then she had her purse zipped shut and was opening the door. "Thanks," she said, not even giving me a glance, "it was sweet of you to do this." And before I knew it, I was out of my truck and heading toward her because she seemed a bit wobbly on her feet. She was clinging to the side of my truck, kind of gripping the door handle. "I can make it," she said. "You better run on home." But I took her arm anyways, gave her elbow a careful tug, and she showed me a weak, miserable smile from that bulging mouth, which didn't appear bad at all with that fresh lipstick and fleshy makeup smeared around it.

To be honest, I'd only seen places like that in movies. There was this faded, velvety wallpaper peeling in the corridor, coming loose above worn, tattered rusty-colored carpet. It was as if crazy couples should be yelling at each other behind them hallway doors, as if gunshots should be going crack crack crack! But instead it was pretty quiet, not even a TV or radio playing loud, and the only noise that I noticed was some old woman mumbling, "Essie, is that you?" from inside her room when me and Ramona went by.

I got to say that I was enjoying helping Ramona the way I was, sort of slick and cool in my mind, with my hand on her arm for support. So when we stopped at her door, I kind of regretted having to let go. And as she fumbled in her purse for the key, I was working on how I'd say goodnight, because for some reason I wanted the words to be perfect. I didn't want her to think I was some idiot kid or that I didn't care about what had happened to her. I mean, I still was feeling pretty lousy about not showing more concern back at the house. The funny thing was, no joke, once she undid the lock and everything, before I could say, "If you need anything, just give me a call," or, "Are you sure you'll be okay," she went, "You want a Coke or something before you go back?"

Her room wasn't much. Old dresser. Funky mattress on the floor. Two metal chairs. A brown scatter rug. Kind of a dump. Over in one corner there was a fridge, this tiny vented stove, a sink. Ramona fixed me up with a Dr Pepper, then went into the bathroom, sort of shutting the door halfway. So I just stood on that scatter rug in the center of that room, sipping on my drink, wondering what would've brought someone like Ramona to the Royal Hotel. I wasn't trying to be a snoop or nothing, but I couldn't help sweeping my eyes around once or twice. There wasn't any kind of things someone might call personal, not pictures or books or even those silly magnets on the fridge, just these skimpy dresses and halters and Wranglers hanging on a suspended rod against one wall. Her bed was a muss of black and rosy satin sheets. That was about it.

Something else, though. As I was nursing that Dr Pepper, waiting for Ramona to finish in the bathroom, I spotted this small rhinestone hairclip on the floor by my boots. So I bent over, picked it up, and just studied it without much in my head. But what happened was, when I moved from that rug to set the clip on the kitchenette counter, I caught a glimpse of Ramona in the bathroom. There I was sort of gazing, and the next thing I know, I'm slipping that hairclip into my pocket.

I know I should've looked away, but I didn't. I don't think I could've if I'd wanted to. I mean, there she was with only that slightly open door between us. She was getting a bottle of pills from the medicine cabinet above the sink. She twisted the cap away, shook a couple of pills to her palm, and then threw them pills into her mouth. Before I knew it, she had the faucet on and was swallowing a handful of water. And as that water was still coming from the spigot, she sort of gazed at her dress in the mirror. And I was going to walk back to that rug again, I really was, but then she had to go pull that dress up by the hem, just yanked it over and off, kind of tossed it behind her. Then down went her slip. And there I was, and there she was. She went about rinsing her face at the sink in just a bra and lace panties, cleaning her skin with a rag, sort of massaging those bruises and bumps, which hit me as being weird because only a few minutes earlier she'd covered her face in fresh lipstick and stuff.

Then, in a flash, I was standing right in the middle of that rug, gulping at the Dr Pepper, glancing everywhere except near that bathroom, kind of pretending that all them clothes on that rod were like the most interesting things I'd ever laid my eyes on. And Ramona was coming toward me, tying a white robe at her waist. And when I turned, I saw that her brown hair was wet and combed straight, that her skin was much darker without that makeup. She appeared sort of fresh and clean, maybe even younger than what I thought. She was saying, "Tell your mom how much I appreciate everything. Now and again I—just—" Then her eyes welled and her voice got all ragged. She started sobbing again, but not quietly this time around.

So I just reached out to squeeze her shoulder through that robe. And when I did that, Ramona leaned forward and put her head on my chest. And all I could think to do was wrap my arms around her, but there wasn't nothing bad about the way I did it. It was the damnedest thing too, because suddenly I'd lost my breath and got uneasy as hell. I mean, I didn't know what to say either, so I kind of lowered my head to where it lightly touched the side of her face. All I could do was just hold her, but for some reason I kept staring down at the top of that Dr Pepper can in my hand as my fingers began crunching around it. It seemed like we was clinging there for a million or so years, almost not moving, like we was about to drown or something. Then she stepped away, wiping them tears with the sleeve of her robe, saying, "You be careful going home, okay?"

"Don't worry about that."

And she tried to smile for real when she asked me, "What's your name again?"

So I smiled with her, going, "Willy. William Keeler," which was pretty dumb considering she knew my mom was Pug Keeler and all.

"Willy," she said, but in a dreamy tone, like she was making sure she'd never forget it. Then before I knew what was happening, Ramona went and kissed my cheek. Just smack. Quick as the wind. Not long or anything, but about long enough to make me never want to go home again.

And that's how it was. I got hooked. Jesus, even when I was walking through that crappy lobby, passing that huge, ungrinning, bloodshot, black clerk behind the front desk, who was reading *Penthouse* as I headed toward the hotel doors, Ramona had my stomach glowing inside. Even as I went by Roughnecks with its beer signs and "Achy Breaky Heart" playing, as I overheard that Bouffant Woman talking to some Western-cut-dress-shirt, slacks-wearing, Stetsoned, alligator-boot-stomping yo-yo, going, "Well, you know the saying, darlin'—it ain't what you *do* for the money, it's what the money'll do for you," Ramona's kiss was still warm on my face.

The drive to Claude was, like my English teacher Mrs. Christian might put it, agreeable. I was wide awake, sort of hyper, had the windows down—forget it's like nearly freezing—with my friend Roy singing, "Sweet dream baby."

And that's how I am now, except it's quiet here. Junie's gone home. Mom hasn't come in. The house is mine, and there's some fried chicken in the kitchen almost screaming for me to get at it.

Dancing the Orange Blossom Special

When Mike Porter comes waltzing in with his sombrero and twanging fiddle, he hollers, "Bullshit," and everyone in the Arb Zane Community Center about goes nuts with applause. That's when the schottische begins. That's when we all get lined up for dancing. That's when Mike Porter and his twin sons Cole (on electric guitar) and Thad (on stand-up bass) rattle the corrugated walls. That's when Mrs. Mike Porter does a little roll with the sticks on this single snare drum.

So there I am looking like the King of America, all fancy and smelling great, in the schottische row with one arm on Hanna, who's Mrs. Wranglers and Boots too, and damn if I don't got my brain on a magazine article Coach Bud gave me before football season. Ain't that the way it is sometimes. I mean, I shouldn't be thinking about nothing more than dancing and Hanna and how good I feel at this very moment. I should be patting myself on the ass because of tonight's game, though there's no need to be a brag or anything. Still, it was like I could do no wrong from the start. On the very first play I took the hand-off, thundered along like a stallion, juked a cornerback, and jogged into the end zone. No problem. The rest of the Homecoming game is too painful to mention, especially when I picture them Guthrie boys on the opposing bench with their frowny faces, their coach screaming and going on like a baby.

Anyway, that article was real strange and interesting to read. It was all about how these scientists were trying to understand this idea of the Zone. They'd brought in all these athletes and asked them all these questions, like what was going through their heads when they couldn't do no wrong on the field or the court or whatever. They called that being in the Zone. Like when Nolan Ryan was pitching a no-hitter, or when Michael Jordan can't miss the hoop even if he's not aiming for it.

This one tennis player said it was like being a human magnet. And this other guy, this baseball player, said there wasn't a way to explain it in normal words. He called it a moment of complete and unspeakable perfection, whatever the hell that means. Then there was a Buddhist fellow from California who talked about archers visualizing where the arrow was going to hit before firing. He taught the archers how to nail the bull's-eye by telling them to aim at themselves in their mind. Now, that's insane. If they'd asked me, I'd have said it's like running through a corridor of open doors that are about to slam shut, one right after the other, and for some reason I know what I got to do is make it past them doors before they close. There ain't an athlete who can make it happen. It just happens when it wants. There ain't a scientist that'll ever make sense of that.

So tonight I was all over the Zone. It was like floating outside of my body and calling the moves to myself an eye-blink before they occurred. I don't mean to sound cocky and all, but Coach Bud tells me it ain't bragging if it's true. All the same, I went out of my way to shake the hands of the Guthrie guys when the game was done, even though a few of them didn't want me anywhere near them.

The most important thing is what I saw from the sideline during the game. Off in the stands was these two guys, one black and one white. And I'd never seen them before either. They stuck out like a pair of Jehovah's Witnesses at a livestock show. They had on these nice coats and slacks. And there was this one time when I got pushed out of bounds by a Guthrie player, so when I looked into the stands I noticed the black guy was writing on this clipboard. Of course, I didn't say nothing to Coach Bud because he gets all worried about scouts screwing with my game. It'd just about drive him over the edge if he knew I saw them there. He'd have to haul me to the sideline and give me that lecture about maintaining my mindset. What he don't seem to understand is that when I'm in the Zone, there ain't nothing short of a bullet that can stop me from flying with that football.

Now the lights are dim in the community center. I'm two-stepping with Hanna and she's got her head on my shoulder. Mike Porter and his family are playing a bluesy, sort of lonesome song he announced as being called "Don't Leave Me." And I keep seeing these couples swim by, all solemn and holding each other. Pug and Stump. Junie and Bob. Lee and Patricia. Sammy and Lilah. Harvey and Liz. And then Ramona comes to my mind, and for a second I pretend it ain't Hanna's body pressing against my chest. Then this voice from behind goes, "Hanna, I need to talk to you," and she slips from me all flustered and a little nervous, like she'd been caught doing something wrong.

"I'll be back," she says, leaving me there by myself on the dance floor. And when I turn I see her walking away with her father, which surprises me some because I've never seen him at a dance before. So I go to the other side of the room and sit down in one of the metal chairs against the wall, which sort of vibrates from the music, and I gaze through them slow-dancing couples to where Mr. Lockhart is bending near Hanna's face and trying to talk over the music. And his jaw keeps going up and down, up and down, and Hanna just nods and nods, her eyes kind of shooting to the sides every so often, like she's worried people are watching her and her father. By the time Mr. Lockhart is done flapping his lips and makes for the door, the community center lights are brighter and Mike Porter has already grabbed the microphone to yell, "Bullshit," once more before launching into something faster and wilder. "The Beer Barrel Polka."

I meet Hanna in the middle of the dance floor. I pull her into me. Then suddenly we're like two spinning tops or something. We're shooting around the concrete floor like a pair of Tasmanian devils in heat, though I ain't got no idea what that's like. Hanna's saying, "Daddy says I can't stay out too late."

"That all?"

"He'd heard there's going to be a party and drinking and he was just worried."

"There ain't no party tonight."

"He's just worried is all."

"He should be."

"What's that supposed to mean, Willy?"

"Nothing. Not a thing."

"Daddy said you played good tonight."

"That's nice," I say, not really meaning it, then I twirl us past Pug and Stump, who ain't dancing as fast as me and Hanna on account of the fact that they're already drunk. Then I grin with the thought that during his pep rally speeches Mr. Lockhart always says, "Win with dignity," and I think me and the team about pulled that one off, except for Sammy, who, after taking a pass into the end zone, hotdogged a moonwalk with the football held out in front of him. I'm sure Mr. Lockhart hated that because he's all into appearances and goes on and on about how others should behave. He also always says, "Lose with confidence," which don't make no sense at all.

It's like one time, when I was only a freshman, me and Lee and Sammy and Harvey were in the school library doing our research for these essays on Shakespeare for Mrs. Christian's class. The four of us found this table on the other side of the library from craggy old Mrs. Doyle, who was the librarian before she died last year from a broken hip that somehow gave her pneumonia. Well, we was supposed to be taking notes and studying passages from *Hamlet* and finding at least three sources for the paper and stuff, but it didn't end up that way.

Lee didn't have his mind on doing studying, and neither did Sammy. But me and Harvey, well, we had our noses in the soliloquy Mrs. Christian assigned, reading that part in the play where Hamlet's walking around feeling all sorry for himself, going, "What a piece of work is man." But I could hear Lee and Sammy ribbing each other. They were whispering and joking around and kind of getting on my nerves. Then Lee went, "Hey, guys," to me and Harvey, and when I glanced across the table I saw Lee pushing back in his chair with that crazy face of his. Then I noticed his Wranglers were unbottoned and the purple head of his dick was peeking through the fly. I mean, it surprised the hell out of me. Sammy was just about to piss himself because he was holding in his laugh. But Harvey just shook his head and said, "Put that germ-infested thing away, Lee." Then Sammy pulled his long pecker out and plopped it down into the middle of that Shakespeare play in his lap, like it was a bookmark or something.

Then Lee climbed from his chair and walked right on over to a shelf of biography books. His face was pretending to be serious and he was acting like he was searching for some important title, but his dick was still poking from his pants. I won't bother to explain what Sammy did with himself after Lee went to the shelf, but I'll mention that by then Harvey had had just about enough. His face was all red, and he grabbed his stuff and left the table saying, "Bunch of dumbass kids," or something similar. As for me, I can't say that I didn't find the whole thing funny, but I was nervous as hell and kept looking over my shoulder to make sure Mrs. Doyle wasn't nearby. I mean, if she'd seen Lee or Sammy that way, she might have keeled over and busted that hip almost two years too soon.

There's a desk in the library where this dictionary called *The New American Standard* sits open on a huge wooden stand. It's like the biggest dictionary in the world. It's so wide that it nearly swallows that whole desktop. It's got this brown leather cover and binding, and if someone tried to lift it they'd think they was carrying a whole set of encyclopedias or something. Anyway, Harvey went and put himself at that desk to get away from Lee and Sammy and their peckers. See, that's the problem with those guys. If they know they're bugging someone, then they'll keep on bugging him until that person wants to kill them.

So Harvey was busy writing notes or whatever, and Lee goes creeping after him. Then Lee's standing beside Harvey and right in front of *The New American Standard*. The thing is, I didn't see what happened next because Sammy was heading toward Harvey and Lee, so my view was blocked. But what I do know is that Lee stretched his dick a little further from his Wranglers and began rubbing it on the pages of that monster dictionary. Then there was a WHOMP! Then I heard a cry, real deep-toned and pained, like Harvey might have gone and lopped Lee's pecker clean off. That cry was so frightening that Sammy, who wasn't quite to where Lee and Harvey were, turned around to face me with an upset expression, like he'd just seen the awfulest thing someone could imagine. Then Sammy was almost running back to our table, zipping his pants, going, "Oh, man, Harvey fixed Lee good," and that's when I spotted Lee hunched across *The New American Standard*, struggling to knock Harvey's pressing hands from the closed leather cover, his dick sandwiched somewhere near the center of that dictionary between Nimrod and Orestes, his legs jerking and bouncing around like he'd just stumbled into an electric fence.

I've seen some pretty ugly things. I mean, crap that makes my stomach just want to let loose of whatever it's got brewing. Perhaps the ugliest two things that come to mind is popping grub worms from cattle and castrating pigs. The grubs are nasty because they don't just pop clean from the cattle, instead they got to come all bloody and mixed with this dirty, stinky puss. And the pigs are even worse because, I swear, they know what's about to be done. Them pigs bellow and kick and carry on, and then once those testicles are snipped, blood squirts all over the place, all over the work gloves, all over a guy's Wranglers and boots. It's a wonder them pigs don't bleed to death. So besides those two things, I'd say the sight of Harvey's psycho smile as he banged his hands on that dictionary, just bang bang bang while Lee's dick was trapped inside, is about the ugliest, most disturbing thing I've ever laid my eyes on.

A guy might have thought Lee would be messed up after that, but he was okay. I mean, once Harvey stopped pounding on that dictionary, Lee scrambled over to the table, his face flushed and angry, zipping his pants like it wasn't no big deal. Jesus, I think me and Sammy were expecting him to be limping or something. "I swear," Lee said, "you wait, Harvey's got his coming," but that's how he is, just talk and more talk.

Anyway, that should've been the end of all that stuff, except somehow word spread around school about what had gone on in the library that afternoon. To be honest, I think Harvey felt so damn good about besting Lee that he blabbed to someone, who blabbed to someone, who blabbed it to the whole of Claude. In this town it don't take much to get people rigored and disgusted about the tiniest of things. By the next morning, there was a creepy kind of quiet at school. It's really hard to explain, so I'll just say it was like in those old Western movies. There's the guy with the white hat and he's just ridden into town, so he goes to the saloon for a drink or something. And everybody in the saloon is talking and there's piano music, but soon as White Hat hits those swinging doors, everything stops. That's how it was when I got to school that morning.

I came down the hallway from my locker and people was whispering when I went past. Mrs. Long and Mrs. Cooke were standing by the water fountain, sort of staring with eyes that said, "You're in a heap of trouble." It really pissed me off because I wasn't the one who'd gone and insulted Shakespeare and Harvey and *The New American Standard* with my pecker.

So then I was in homeroom and before I could even sit, Mr. Lockhart's voice crackles from the intercom, "Teachers, will you please excuse all the high school boys from class. I need to speak with them in the auditorium." And dammit if I wasn't scared. I don't know why, but I really was.

Next thing I knew, there I was in the auditorium. And it's me and Sammy and Lee and Harvey and all the other guys. And there wasn't any teachers or nobody except Mr. Lockhart, and he's standing on the stage above us, like he's in a play or something, and I kept expecting him to say, "Murder most foul," or to point his fingers and go, "For murder, though it have no tongue, will speak with most miraculous organ," which would've been pretty funny. But instead he went, "I don't need to tell you boys how disappointed I am in you," and that was real goofy because the only people he should've been yapping at was Lee and Sammy and Harvey. But Mr. Lockhart ain't that way. He's always saying, "If one person makes this school look bad, it makes all of us look bad," and silly shit like that.

So for almost an hour he went on and on about hygiene and personal cleanliness and how when we do things that we think no one sees, we're only lying to ourselves, because someone always sees it. "There's just behavior that we do as children that we regret as men," he said, "and I think some of you know what I'm talking about." And I swear to God he was looking straight at me when those words came from his mouth. And then he told us all to think hard on what he'd just talked about, and then he instructed us to leave the auditorium single file and without saying a word. The stupid thing was, none of us knew for sure what in hell he'd been talking about. He never got to the point. He never even mentioned what had happened in the library.

And soon as we were out of that auditorium, Lee leaned over my shoulder and kind of whispered, "What goes on in that man's head?" And if I wasn't so nervous about Mr. Lockhart seeing me, I'd have probably grinned or said something like, "There ain't nothing but static going on in that man's head."

Mike Porter goes, "This'll be our last go-around tonight, folks, so get your boots scraping." And then here comes the "Orange Blossom Special," except I'm too tired to hit the dance floor. Even Hanna's bushed. We're in two of them metal chairs against the wall. She's got her head slumped against my neck, and I got my head resting on her hair, which sort of stinks from all that junk she sprays in it. There are about four couples left dancing. And even though Mike Porter and his family have been at it for nearly three hours, they still appear wide awake and happy on their instruments.

Next thing I know, Lee's coming into the community center. He's sort of staggering some. I can tell he's drunk. He ain't got his shirt on. He's just Wranglers and boots and baseball cap, and he's rubbing his arms because it's freezing outside. When he spots me and Hanna, he gives us a sloppy wave and comes ambling over to where we're sitting. "Why ain't you dancing," he asks.

"Too tired," I tell him. "Where's Patricia?"

"Bitch pissed me off."

"You're drunk," I say.

"No I ain't."

"Where's your shirt?"

"Bitch tore it. Come on, Hanna, why don't you dance with me."

"No thanks."

"This one dance."

"No thanks, Lee."

Then Lee steps right in front of me. "Let's dance," he says, which just about cracked me up.

"With you?"

"Come on, people, it's the 'Orange Blossom Special'!"

Then he grabs my arm and practically yanks me from my seat. "Goddammit, Lee!"

"It ain't nothing," he tells me. "You ain't a fag, right?"

"You know I ain't."

"I ain't a fag."

"I know."

"Then there ain't nothing wrong with it. You can lead."

So I glance at Hanna. She's giving me this look that says, "Don't you dare," which is like the worst look someone can give me.

"It's the 'Orange Blossom Special,'" I tell her.

"You two deserve each other," she says.

Then I put one hand on Lee's waist and off we go. And I'm laughing so hard it hurts. And I ain't the only one. Just about everyone left in the place is roaring too. I mean, all them couples on the floor sort of stop and give us room, and I hear Mike Porter go, "Ain't love a beautiful thing."

"It truly is," Lee yells, and I can smell the beer from his mouth. I feel my palms warming his cold skin, and we're swinging around so fast that my head gets dizzy.

2:36:57 A.M.

My watch is broken, I guess. Every so often I push the button that shines this little light on the numbers, and it's always the same time. When I fell on the walkway, my arms hit kind of hard on the metal, so maybe that's how it got busted. Of course, there's this bitter wind up here, so maybe the freeze just zapped the battery or something. Or maybe when Hanna was kicking at me with her boots, she nailed my watch and it started slowing then. I don't know.

What's strange is how one night Joel woke me. Out of the blue he told me nothing can escape from a black hole. "Not even light," he said. "In a black hole time kind of stops. A single second gets stretched out forever, so it's like there ain't no time at all." I guess he was having a bad dream or something, or he couldn't get to sleep. So he started going on about how he kept thinking about these black holes in the universe, and he said it was sort of bothering him that they were out there somewhere. I swear, the damnedest things come from his mouth when he can't sleep.

So I said to him, "Don't worry. There ain't no black holes going to get us," and that seemed to make him feel better for some reason. To be honest, I don't know nothing about all that stuff. But now I'm wondering about them black holes. I'm wondering what if one just decided to suck in Claude and everyone with it, then maybe everybody's watch would quit. Maybe that's why my watch don't work now.

Anyway, nights like this I don't want to go home. It ain't that I'm not tired or nothing. I am. It's just that I need to be somewhere other than my bed. It's like I can't think straight there, and I'd probably not get much sleep anyway.

My right palm is bleeding a bit from when I climbed across the barbed wire, and then I slipped on some ice on the catwalk. For a second I thought I was about to slide from the water tower and go hurtling into space. I'm sure I'd have been bellowing and kicking. I bet I'd have ended all tangled and torn in those barbed-wire coils on that fence down there.

William Keeler, dead at eighteen. Tiger football star found mangled and gross in what may have been a suicide jump.

That really would be something, huh?

Then everybody would be upset. There wouldn't be no school for two or three days. Hanna would be a total wreck. All she would think about was how she should've done it with me tonight after the dance. She'd spend hours alone in her room, just crying and hugging my picture. She'd go over our last moments together in her mind, and she'd wish she hadn't kicked at me tonight in my truck. She'd imagine us embracing on the seat, my body on top of her, and she'd change it all around. She'd let me tug at her pants instead of telling me to stop. And once I got them pants almost down to her hips, she'd relax as I pushed her shirt up so I could touch her stomach and put my fingers under her bra. She wouldn't struggle like she did, even as I tried to yank harder on her pants to get them to her knees. She just wouldn't get all tense and frantic, and she wouldn't kick at me so I'd get off her.

To be honest, it about drives me insane sometimes. I know it ain't right what I did, but there's just this thing in me that wants her so bad. I mean, it ain't like she don't want it, or why else would she let it all go so damn far? If she'd just let me inside she'd know. It kind of spooks me when I get feeling that way, but I just want to fucking take her and stick it in. Then she'd see how good it can be. But I know it's wrong like that. I really do. But sometimes I get sort of excited when I think how wild that'd be to do it that way. I don't know why I get like that.

Actually, I feel sort of like a jerk about what happened. When she said, "You could've torn my shirt," her voice had a tremble, and all I did was shrug and stare out the windshield like a goof. I wasn't nearly as mad as I looked. It was like when she scooted over next to me, I could tell that she was nervous, but I didn't know what to say. "I'm sorry," she told me. "I just—we just can't—"

When I took her home, I noticed how all the lights were off in her house. And that got me wondering about something Hanna once told me. She said sometimes she gets home and Mr. Lockhart is waiting for her in the dark. He's just sitting in his recliner chair and waiting. And this one night she came home and closed the door behind her. Then she reached for the wall switch to click on the living room light. That's when she heard Mr. Lockhart go, "Leave it off," which almost made Hanna jump clean from her boots. So she said, "Daddy—" and tried to spot him in all that blackness.

She said she gazed into the shadows and barely saw him. There he was in that recliner with his pipe glowing. And if that ain't creepy enough, when she asked him what he was doing, he went, "Waiting for you."

Then she said something like, "Why? I'm not that late." And when he didn't say anything to her, she sort of whispered, "Daddy—?"

So then he went, "Go to bed, Hanna. I think you should just—" and then his voice just stopped. She told me she stood there for a long time after that. She told me she was scared to step forward for some reason. And when she finally did move, she almost slammed into a wall because it was so dark, and because she was sort of running to get to her room.

There was another thing too. It didn't seem so bad then, but it kind of tosses my guts now. I mean, there we were in the Lockharts' backyard on a Saturday. It was me and Hanna and Sammy. And we was just enjoying ourselves there among those hedges and flower beds and them three cottonwood trees, except for some reason I was in a funk about something. I can't even remember what now. I was stretched out on the grass, sort of being moody under one of them trees. But Hanna and Sammy were having fun. They were throwing this football back and forth, and Sammy kept acting dumb when he caught the ball. He'd run around saying, "No one can stop me! No one can stop me!" and Hanna would try to catch him. It's kind of hard to explain how funny that was.

Anyway, as they were playing, Sammy swivel-hipped toward Hanna, who grabbed on to one of his legs. The two of them dragged along some, and then they collapsed next to me under the tree. Then Hanna bent over and stared right into my eyes. But like I said, I was in some sort of grumpy place. She was kind of studying me with a smiling look, and then she kissed me on the forehead. And Sammy went, "Turn the frog into a prince!" So when I didn't react or nothing, Hanna took this stem of grass and tickled my nose with it. So I brushed her hand away. Next thing I knew, I was grabbing her around the waist, and she called out for Sammy to help her. Pretty soon the three of us was wrestling around and acting like kids, and Hanna was screaming too. Then I climbed on top of her and held her wrists. Then Sammy found a bit of grass and started tickling her lips with it. That's when I saw him.

I mean, Hanna and Sammy didn't know Mr. Lockhart was watching us, but I did. And for some reason I was enjoying the fact that I was holding Hanna's shoulders to the ground while Sammy hovered over her with that grass blade. And she was breathing hard and laughing and bouncing her waist between my legs, and Mr. Lockhart was at the kitchen window. I don't think I've ever caught sight of a face so hard or angry. He appeared like the bunched end of a sausage. And for a moment the two of us was eye-to-eye, except he was pissed crazy and I was shit-eating from one side of my mouth to the other.

Now that I'm thinking about Mr. Lockhart and how he is, I'm getting downright depressed about everything. I got all this crap going on in my brain. Sometimes it ain't there at all. Sometimes it's filling my thoughts, all gray and murky. It don't make much sense. It's like how them two northern flicker woodpeckers at NASA went and gouged a billion holes into the *Atlantis*. Go figure, right? I mean, there they are, all set and everything to launch that shuttle on this historic docking mission with a Russian space station. Those scientists calculated all kinds of things, like how to get the shuttle up there, how to get it back, what happens if a booster blows, shit like that. And then them two woodpeckers decided they need to go banging all over the insulation on a fifteen-story fuel tank. Just out of nowhere they came, screwing up months of planning by the best minds on the planet, and suddenly all that technology and all those calculations didn't mean squat. Stuff like that about turns me crazy. So that's why I'm here, I guess, because soon as I think I got a handle on things, all of a sudden I don't. Forget that my body is chilled throughout, or that my nose keeps on dripping. I just need to put some distance between me and all that stuff down there.

When I was heading this way in my truck, I was wanting to stay up here until morning. But now I don't know what time it is, so I could be here forever. Still, I got my boots hanging into space. I got my arms folded together on the railing, and Claude ain't nothing more than a few hundred fluorescent lights hanging over them dim streets. There ain't no houses I can spot. I can't even really see the ground. It's like if I had Stump's rifle with the scope, I could sit here and just shoot out them streetlights. I'd just shoot them until there was nothing below me except darkness. I'd be sitting right here and Claude would just be a gaping black hole in the middle of another black hole.

TWO

TWO

Ode

It's like one minute life seems nothing but nothing, and then the next minute, something happens and life gets to being unexpected and sort of fantastic. It's like one minute I was raising my hand in Mr. Elder's Computer Math class to ask if I could be excused, and the next minute I was in mid-piss and Bess, who's our school's secretary, came on the overhead speaker with, "Willy Keeler, come to the office please, right now."

Soon as I stepped into that office, Bess pushed this phone at me, and I didn't know what the hell to think. She was kind of hyper and all smiley. She had her hand cupped on the talking end of the phone. Her lips were twitching. She was so excited that it took the words a moment to spill out. Then finally she went, "It's for you! It's Ode Newhouse with the Dallas Cowboys! And I talked to him! But he wants to talk to you!"

That about floored me. To be honest, I thought it was some joke. I thought Coach Bud or Lee or even Stump might be having me on. But I took that phone anyway, except I took it real slow. I mean, I was hesitant to put that receiver to my head. Then I sort of listened to see what I could hear, except I didn't hear anything. So then I just said, "Hello—?"

And then a low, low voice said, "Is this *the* Willy Keeler?"

I about shit myself. "Yes, sir," I said, "it is."

"This is Ode Newhouse. How you doing, man?"

"Okay, I think. Is this really Newhouse?"

"Yeah, this is the man! I wanted to rap with you a minute. That okay?"

"Sure." Like I was going to say anything else. By then my hands were shaking. I was kind of having a hard time breathing, and dammit if Bess didn't just stand there staring at me. That nearly drove me goofy. I mean, she had no idea what Newhouse was talking about, but she kept nodding her head like she was part of the conversation.

"I hear a multitude of good things about you," he was saying. "I hear you're kicking ass all over the place out there in—" and then his voice quit. And I got all nervous that the line had got disconnected or something. Then I heard papers shuffle around. Then he sort of sighed.

"Claude," I said, trying not to sound snotty or nothing.

"That's right. I keep hearing about the things you've been doing in Claude—"

"Thank you, sir."

"But I want you to do me a favor, okay?"

"Sure—"

"I hear you're thinking on going to Oklahoma. Please tell me that ain't true."

That really screwed with me, because I hadn't heard from Oklahoma yet, even though I figured that was where them two scouts was from. "I don't know," I told him.

"You don't want to leave Texas, man! You don't want any redshirting, or waiting around for your turn, do you?"

"No, sir."

"How'd you like to know you'd be starting as a freshman, huh? Man, I'm talking a starter as a freshman!"

"Well, yeah, I—"

And it struck me just then that those awesome hands of his, those two humongous black hands that caught Archie Hansen's famous zero-second pass in the conference championship, were on the other end of the line. This was the same Ode Newhouse from the Burger Hut commercials: "Burger Hut, because it's *that* good!" He's the same guy whose picture is on my bedroom wall next to Joel's wombats. That about frazzled my brain then. I mean, not three days ago I'd seen a TV news show called *Amer-*

ican Exclusive, and they had this story about Newhouse and his ex-wife, the supermodel Tanya Borgmen. It seems that last year he got drunk and knocked in her front door. Then he beat the shit out of Tanya's boyfriend, and he even punched her too. I couldn't believe it. They had the 911 call and everything.

Tanya: "He's gone crazy!"

911: "Okay, just stay calm. Where is he now?"

Ode: "Put the phone down, bitch!"

And now today, there I was on the phone with him. That's what I mean about life being one thing and then another thing. That's what makes me think there's a God or something.

"Let me tell you, Willy," Ode was telling me. "My good friend Doug is cranking up a hell of a program at SMU, and you'd fit right in. You know how well connected Doug is with the pros? Hell, he played for the Giants! You remember that? I tell you what, man. Roll with Doug, and in four years you're writing your own ticket!"

"I appreciate it, but my coach is—"

"Hey, man, let me tell you something. Your coach is going to stay right there where he is. *You're* the one going places. Understand me?"

So I said, "Yes, sir," even though I didn't like the way he'd said all that. I mean, I know it was Ode Newhouse and all, but he just doesn't got any idea of Coach Bud and me.

"Willy, I'm going to tell Doug you'll talk to him, okay? I'll personally keep an eye on things. You call me if you need anything. Shit, we'll get you over here to the Cowboys' camp for some workouts this summer."

That was when I almost wanted to holler and jump and stuff. "That'd be great," I told him.

"We'll get you ready like you won't believe. What do you say?"

"Yeah, sure, I guess so."

"Hey, I appreciate it, man. Could be the best thing ever came along for you. I mean it! Doug works real good with black players. He understands *us!*"

I had to crack a wild grin about that. I mean, I was all beside myself because one of my heroes actually knew who I was, and then he went off and showed he didn't know I ain't black. Still, it didn't really bother me none. I just went ahead and nodded and said, "Sounds great."

"That's my man! You hang loose, and don't sign until you hear from Doug, okay?"

"Okay."

"We'll be in touch, right?"

"You bet."

"Take care now."

"You too."

"Bye."

"Bye."

When I handed the phone to Bess, she about yelled, "Well, what'd he say?"

See, that's how she is. In fact, me and Lee call her Busy Bess on account of the fact that she's always putting her nose in everyone's business. She's about the biggest snoop in Claude, and she's an even bigger fibber. Her hair is about ten times wider than her head, and it's got a white streak through the middle. "Skunky," is what Lee says when we pass her in the halls. "Hey, Skunky, what's the news," he'll ask, and she don't got no idea he's making fun of her hair. I swear to God, that woman hatches some of the wildest yarns. And what drives me and Lee over the hill is that most folks believe her. She'll spin her tales at Critter's Beauty & Nail while getting her hair inflated, and by that afternoon the whole of Claude is buzzing with her nonsense:

"Did you hear they're going to build a nudist colony outside of Washburn?"

"Don't tell no one I told you this, but you know how Mrs. Campbell has been in the hospital over in Amarillo? Well, she ain't there for her heart condition, she's there because a three-foot tapeworm slipped from her when she was washing dishes."

"The reason Ed Schaffer's Jacuzzi business went under in

Childress was on account of the fact that a boy there sat down on the drain of one of them whirlpool baths Ed sold and had his insides sucked from him. Now there's a lawsuit pending."

That's the kind of crap she creates. It comes straight from them twitchy lips. Suddenly, there ain't a household in Claude that don't know about nudist clubs, monster tapeworms, or butt-sucking hot tubs. There's about a million others too. There's probably a ton of stuff she's blabbed and I'm carrying it around as God's truth.

Lee calls her the Devil's radio, but he only says that because that's how Brother McColey describes her. I mean, Brother McColey don't like Busy Bess at all, and he nearly says as much in his sermons. I expect he's still mad about all that business with him and Mrs. Dunn. It was Bess who caught them in the act, just naked and horndog as can be in the baptismal pit. They were splashing around in the water, doing whatever it was they was doing, and Bess, who'd stopped by First Baptist one afternoon to pick up a pan she'd forgot at the last covered-dish supper, happened to catch it all through this stained-glass window. Claude almost went psycho over that one. I think it'd have been a lot worse if both Brother McColey and Mrs. Dunn hadn't been widowed. Still, there's something kind of filthy about screwing in the baptismal pit. That just don't seem right.

Anyway, Bess was going, "Well, what'd he say, Willy? What'd Ode Newhouse say?"

"It's a secret," I said, bringing a finger and a thumb to my mouth. "It'd ruin everything if I told." Then I zipped my lips with that finger and that thumb, and Bess got all frowny.

"I know what he said," she told me. "I was right here. His voice was as clear as could be." But by then I'd already turned around and was walking from the office.

So now I'm in the playground, except I should be back in Computer Math. All I can hear is the chains clinking on the swings when the wind blows. I'm sitting in the sandbox and the playground is empty. I'm writing my name again and again in the sand. Writing it like an autograph. And twice I've written Ode Newhouse's name too, putting it right next to my name. And I'm imagining him in slacks and a green Polo shirt and loafers. He's seated in a large swivel-chair behind a sprawling desk, with his feet propped and the receiver of a telephone cradled under his chin. And he's saying my name as I scratch it in the sand.

Ragweed Fever Head

It ain't so much my body, but my head and my eyes and my nose are all crummy. It's like my eyes itch something terrible. I got a headache. My nose can't make up its mind; one nostril is clogged to my brain, the other nostril runs like the Salt Fork of the Brazos. And I'm tired as hell. I just want to go home, get undressed, and disappear under them sheets. God, the thought of driving home makes me want to konk out right now. "Might be a case of ragweed," Coach Slick mentioned to me as we was jogging from the school to the practice field. "It's going around. It's getting at me."

"Ah, he's just nervous," Coach Bud said, because he knew I was pretty worried about my first meeting with Ben Denton, who was waiting at the field when we got there.

Now the whole team is running through plays on one end of the field with Coach Slick, while Coach Bud and me and Ben Denton and this old hippie photographer Ben keeps calling Hotshot are by the bleachers. And Hotshot has a tattered camera bag slung over a shoulder. He's got a red bandana tied about his forehead. His long nasty hair looks like it ain't ever been washed. He's wearing a vest that has all these pouches on it for film and stuff, I guess. He's sort of hovering around with his 35mm camera, clicking shots of me and Coach Bud as Ben talks to us.

I mean, here I am feeling all gross and scratchy and achy, and I'm supposed to be real calm and confident on account of the fact that Ben is the sportswriter for the *Amarillo Daily News*. He's got his small reporter's pad flipped open. He's jotting notes. He's saying, "You expect this story to bring in more offers?"

So I go, "Well, it's an honor, but I don't really know about that—"

Then Hotshot practically gets in my face. He's so close to me that I snort a whiff of his body odor. He's adjusting the lens, and his funky gray hair keeps falling across the camera. Then CLICK! Then CLICK CLICK! And Ben says, "When AP puts you in the top twenty prospects in the state—that's pretty good company."

I swear to Jesus my mind ain't working so well at the moment. Old Hotshot is sort of crowding me. Ben's mouth is moving so fast I hardly understand what he's going on about, and there's a dusty breeze scooting over the practice field. I hear myself say, "I appreciate that they—think that—but without my coach, my team, I—I couldn't be there—" and I glance at Coach Bud and he don't appear so happy.

Then CLICK CLICK CLICK! And Ben says, "Where you going to play?"

And I shrug. Then I recall how Coach Bud said, "Don't shrug off any question Ben throws at you. It don't seem professional." Next thing I know, Coach Bud steps right between me and Ben, and Hotshot goes CLICK CLICK! And Coach Bud sort of gives this fake grin and says, "We really don't know yet, Ben. We honestly don't."

One of Ben's eyebrows shoots up. He gives Coach Bud an expression that most of us would be scared to give him. It's the kind of look that goes, "You're full of it," but that ain't what comes from Ben. Instead he says, "You're on the level?"

And that fake grin Coach Bud has gets bigger and wider until his face seems like it might just rip apart. "On the level," he tells Ben.

Last night, when I was at Coach Bud's house, he said, "I know you ain't ever had one of these press boys talk to you, but it's as easy as you can imagine. They ask the obvious kind of questions, and you answer with what they want to hear. It's that simple, Willy."

We was in the kitchen and he was frying these huge hamburger patties in a skillet. He had on this greasy apron he always likes to wear when he's cooking. It has a big bald eagle on the front, colored red, white, and blue. And that eagle has its beak ready to chomp down on this red cookie shaped like a star. And standing off away from that cookie is some Asian chef who's frowning mad. And written all over that apron in red, white, and blue is the words *America Will Eat You!* Coach Bud just loves that apron.

That's another thing about Coach Bud, he likes to cook. Mrs. Warfield just stays in the living room doing her knitting and watching TV, and he makes dinner for her and him most every night. "He ain't so macho," Mrs. Warfield once told me when I was sitting at their dining table, and that about bugged Coach Bud to no end.

"Hell, what's preparing a meal got to do with not being macho," he asked, though he was only half joking.

Then she said something like, "Good Lord, Bud, I was just kidding," and then she gave me this little wink when he wasn't looking. I thought that was pretty funny.

Anyway, Coach Bud was frying these specialty hamburgers he'd learned to make when him and Mrs. Warfield were living in New Mexico. He calls them El Gringo Gotchas. Them hamburgers are the best. He mixes them with onions and garlic, then he cooks them with chili powder. Then right before they're done, he puts this white cheese and strips of green chili on them. Like I said, they're the best.

So while Coach Bud was flipping them patties around the skillet, he started telling me how I should act with Ben: "Just be yourself, son. He's going to ask you about how you feel being a top-twenty prospect, and you tell him the truth. How do you feel about being a top-twenty prospect?"

"Good."

"Now, that ain't the kind of thing you need to be saying, Willy. You need to come out with something more creative. This is print. Just good don't look good in print."

So I said, "Being a top-twenty prospect is great for me. It makes me feel good. Really good."

And then he got all moody. He started flipping them patties quicker and quicker. "That won't cut it," he told me. "Son, ain't you ever watched the big boys on TV?"

"Sure."

"And what kind of things do they say?"

The funny thing was, I couldn't remember a damn word those guys said. All I could see was their faces. That's it. They all had those sly faces when being interviewed after a win. Or they had those serious and thoughtful faces after having been beaten. But what they said just didn't stick in my head. Then I recalled how sometimes they just screamed. Some TV guy would shove a microphone at them after some victory, and them players would be in the locker room or on the sideline just yelling like it was the end of the world. "I guess they just like to holler and stuff," I told Coach Bud, but he just shook his head. He bounced them patties around some. He breathed in all deep through his nose.

Then after I had me two of them El Gringo Gotchas, and after Mrs. Warfield showed off a red and green sweater with these tiny bells on the sleeves she's been sewing as a Christmas gift for someone, me and Coach Bud went on out to his garage. He has these two lawn chairs set up in there. He's got them on this square patch of AstroTurf. There's a huge heat lamp hanging down over them chairs from the ceiling. "My winter backyard," he told me.

Pretty soon I was comfortable and warm in that lawn chair, feeling all stuffed and satisfied. Then Coach Bud started feeding me ideas on how to handle myself for the interview. "Just be sure of yourself," he was saying. "Ben Denton is a sharp fellow, but he's fair. Just answer in full sentences, and make sure you get me and the team mentioned a few times in there. It don't sit well if you don't do that, know what I mean?"

I probably should've been paying better attention, but I was so full on them hamburgers, plus I'd had me a big hunk of cobbler, that all I really wanted to do was crash.

"Sure, Coach," I kept saying. "Sure, Coach."

Then he stopped being all hyper about Ben and about how important this interview was going to be for me. He sat forward in his lawn chair as a whole different person. His brow was all scrunched. His eyes were all squinty. He went, "I heard about your phone call from Newhouse."

I mean, Coach Bud had that unsmiling mouth like I've seen right before he hits the roof about something. Right out of the blue it came. One second, he was my best pal, just grins and talky. Next second, he seemed about ready to pounce on me. He got me so nervous that I wasn't sure what to do. It was like my lips were just moving without me thinking. "He just called," I said, all quiet. I sort of had to stare at my boots because I couldn't stand to see his face like that. "I didn't know what to say," I told him.

To be honest, I figured I was about to get the full Coach Warfield treatment. I figured he was about to stretch his jaw and let me have it. But he didn't. Instead he frowned some. Then he went, "Son, do you know how it works? Newhouse makes a nice little bundle making them calls. He's got a list with the names and numbers of football players like yourself. Soon as he's done talking to one, he scratches a line through that kid's name, checks his list for the next name, and makes another call. He ain't doing it because he cares a damn about you and your future. He's doing it for money. There ain't nothing worse than a man who toys with kids just so he can pad his pocket."

"I didn't know he was going to call," I said.

Then Coach Bud got an edge in his tone. He said, "What I've told you is, you let me deal with the dealers! Right? Some of those pricks will shuck you any way they can. Now, am I going to handle things for us or not?"

I'd be lying if I said I wasn't a bit hurt or confused. It wasn't like I'd done anything wrong or anything. What kind of idiot doesn't talk to Ode Newhouse when he calls? But I felt bad because I hadn't told him, and because I know he's just looking out for me. So I went, "Sure, Coach, I'm sorry." And when I glanced up, half expecting to see that crinkled expression, I noticed that his face had softened.

"Willy, I just don't want them taking you down any primrose. That's all." And that was it. Even faster than he'd jumped from Ben Denton to Ode Newhouse, he was back to Ben Denton again. "Anyway, we got that press boy coming tomorrow, so you think you're ready?"

"I think so."

"Good." He slapped my leg. "This calls for something special." Next thing I knew, he'd gone from his lawn chair and was digging around in this old tackle box on the other side of the garage. Then he returned with a plastic sandwich bag that looked like it had skinny turds in it, except it wasn't turds but cigars. And Coach Bud's fingers were fishing two of them cigars out. "Not a word to no one," he said.

It didn't take us long to get those things fired. We just sat in those lawn chairs puffing a storm. That whole damn garage reeked. The smoke just filled the place, all gray and thick and swirly. I kept imagining it was fog, like in those movies with that English detective guy. Anyway, Coach Bud was telling me about how when he retires he's going to buy a cabin in Colorado. He said it'd be right on a river, so all he'd have to do in the mornings was hang his fishing line from the bedroom window. "Up there in Colorado, near Crested Butte, the fish practically jump into your net. Hell, you don't even need a pole!"

And I would've really been enjoying that cigar and listening to him carry on, but all that smoke was making my stomach get weird. My head was becoming sort of light. Them hamburgers weren't sitting so good then. I think Coach Bud saw that I was appearing kind of ill, because he got up and lifted that garage door. Suddenly all the smoke whooshed around and started disappearing. And this cold rush of air came in to where I sat. By then I'd let my cigar burn down to almost nothing.

Coach Bud was just standing a few feet away with his ass to me, and he was staring from that garage opening into the sky. "It's a clear night," he said. "Clear as day." Then he was quiet for a time. Then he went, "Willy, you're the core. No dishonor to the others. They're all damn good players, but you're the one who makes it happen." And he said that, all low and almost weary sounding, without even glancing to me, like I wasn't there or something.

So I said, "Thanks, Coach," but it came from me sort of weak and raggedy on account of what my insides were doing.

Then he turned around, and I swear to God he seemed a bit weepy, though I ain't sure now. "I know I don't say it enough, but you're the core, son." The funny thing was, I'd heard Coach Bud say that about a million times before, except not so personal.

This is how it went before practice and the interview. It was one of them private meetings. Coach Bud likes those best. He gets me and Sammy and Lee and Harvey together with Coach Slick. He gets the four of us players together on account of the fact that he figures us to be the heart of the team: "You boys are the core. No dishonor to the others. They're all damn good kids, but you're the fellows who make it happen."

The four of us sort of stood in front of his desk in our workout pants and T-shirts. We didn't have no top pads on or nothing like that. Coach Slick was leaning against a wall, picking at his teeth with a toothpick. Coach Bud was giving us his speech about Lefors, because he goes way back with Effie, who's the Lefors football coach. The two of them went to UT together, and even though they was good friends then, they ain't so tight now.

What I do know is that Effie and Coach Bud was once so close they gave each other tattoos. I swear to God. Coach Bud told me the whole yarn. That was when they was in college. They got drunk on some stuff called muscatel. Then they got this kind of screwdriver thing with three needles on the end, which was used for putting tattoos in the ears of cattle. They also got a bottle of Army ink. Coach Bud went about putting the initials ETP on the front of Effie's leg with that screwdriver thing. Then Effie took it and put the initials BRW on Coach Bud's thigh, except he was so drunk that it got done all whompyjawed and ugly. Coach Bud said he should've used a stencil to guide Effie's hand. But that wasn't what busted their friendship. Slick told me last year that Effie and Mrs. Warfield had been sweethearts back then, and old Coach Bud sort of won her over. At least that's what Slick told me, but I've been sworn not to say nothing about it. Anyway, that was a long time ago, though Effie still smarts some, I guess.

"What I don't like, boys," Coach Bud was telling us, "is what Effie's liable to try on us. I know him. I know his pea-brained way of coaching! Since Effie's been at Lefors, and we been at the top, all he wants to do is beat Claude. It's personal. Tomorrow night is his whole season. He'll come on with every trick he ever heard of. He's a nasty man and I don't like him. He's got that ol' lardass tackle—" Then he gave Harvey a wink and went, "No offense, Harve," which got us all laughing, even Harvey, who takes ribbing about his weight pretty well. And then the grin slipped from Coach Bud's face as he said, "They're going to do a lot of stunting so their big man can get blind shots at Lee and Willy."

So Harvey piped in with, "Shit, Coach, I can—"

But Coach Bud just waved him off. "Dammit, son, I know what you can do! But it ain't going to be head-on with them. I'm here telling you that with this bunch we're going to have to outcall them!" Then he tapped his forehead with a finger. He tapped himself so hard that I could hear his skin thudding. "We're going to need to think! It ain't going to be our kind of football! We've been over this, I know, but I'm telling you again, boys! I don't give a damn what we're running, Harvey's got to key their big man all night! I don't care if he's at the concession stand, you're there with him, Harvey! You got it?"

So Harvey nodded, but he nodded like a little kid, all slow with big eyes. Then Coach Bud stopped tapping on his forehead, and I noticed this sort of red circle on his brow where his finger had banged. Then Coach Bud aimed that finger right at Lee. "Lee's got to stick with the quick hitters, toss sweeps, and short counts."

Then that finger swung to Sammy, who kind of cringed at the sight of it. "Sammy, you keep an eye on Lee and break them patterns like a matchstick!"

And then it was my turn, except for when that finger came my way, it sort of bent some, and Coach Bud's voice, which had been all harsh, got friendly and almost pleasant. "You use the sidelines, son," he told me. "Don't try to take them all on by yourself. We'll let Calvin gut them now and then to keep them honest, but it probably won't help a damn. We got the rest of our team out there. You boys know I love them, but they ain't shit for football players. You boys are my studs, I mean it, and I'm banking on you."

Then that finger joined the rest of his fingers, and he brought his hands to the desk. For a moment he just shook his head like he was upset about something. Then he said, "I don't like Lefors, but we have to play them if we're going to get where we're going. So let's have a strong practice, get rest tonight, be ready for tomorrow."

And that's usually how them private meetings end, except this time, as I was heading into the locker room with the others, Coach Bud went, "Could you hold a minute, Willy?" So I about-faced and he sort of pointed me into one of them chairs in front of his desk. Then he glanced over at Coach Slick, who was still poking at his teeth with that toothpick. He was digging so far in his mouth I thought he must have stuck his whole damn lunch in there. Anyway, Coach Bud told Coach Slick, "Why don't you make sure the boys don't mess around when they should be warming up," but he didn't say it in a rotten way or nothing, even though it was clear as can be he wanted this to be an extra-private meeting, meaning just me and him. So Coach Slick went on into the locker room, his fist almost stuffed in his mouth, and closed the door behind him.

Then Coach Bud kind of nodded at me. He went, "This is the big one. Ben Denton is already down at the field waiting. Now, I know you're nervous about all this, so I put together this little list. I think it might help keep you on track." He pushed a sheet of paper across the desk to me. "Look it over. Memorize it. All you'll need to know is there."

So I took that paper and began studying what he'd written on it:

YOU FEEL IT'S AN HONOR TO BE A PROSPECT
YOU'RE LEARNING
YOU'RE IMPROVING
YOU HAVE A NO-NONSENSE APPROACH TO THE GAME
YOU PLAY WITH EMOTION
GIVE CREDIT TO THE COACHES
GIVE CREDIT TO THE TEAM
YOU'RE GOOD AND GETTING BETTER

"Make sense to you?" he said.
"Yes, sir," I told him.

Now I'm sitting on the first row of the bleachers.

I've about wiped a gallon of snot on the shoulder of my practice jersey. Coach Bud is finishing up the interview with Ben. Hotshot is standing nearby and taking the film from his camera. Ben is saying, "We've given Claude and Willy a lot of space, and I want the word on him first."

And Coach Bud goes, "You'll have it, Ben, don't worry."

"I damn sure don't want to read it on the wires, Coach. I want this one."

"You'll have it when we decide. I promise you."

Then Ben sort of looks past Coach Bud and says to me, "You got anything else to say, big guy?"

So I go, "It's just an honor to be a prospect. I'm learning. I'm improving. Coach has taught me a no-joking way to play the game, so I play real seriously. If it weren't for Coach and Coach Slick and the team, I wouldn't be good and getting better."

Then Coach Bud's face brightens. He gives me a little nod that says, "There you go."

Ben starts taking notes like he's just heard the most amazing thing in the world and doesn't want to forget it.

Then Hotshot drops down beside me, and I inhale his stink again with my one good nostril. He's dusting off his camera. Coach Bud and Ben begin walking away on the sideline. Coach Bud slips an arm across Ben's shoulders. The wind is whooshing around so much that I can't hear what they're telling each other. Hotshot stares at me, then he stares across the field. "It's getting nasty," he says. "Don't seem right for this time of year," and at first I don't know what the hell he's talking about. So I just follow his gaze and spot a big old dust cloud, all rusty and spooky, creeping toward Claude. I figure it's about ten miles or so outside of town, maybe closer. Then Hotshot has his camera bag open. He's suddenly loading that camera with more film. Then he goes, "Hey, kid, do me a favor."

"What?"

"Go stand out in the middle of the field."

So I push off the bleacher and go several yards until Hotshot yells, "That's good. Now face me. That's great."

And he's CLICK CLICK CLICKING like crazy. I'm somewhere between Hotshot and that monster wall of dust. I put my hands on my thighs. I sort of squint my eyes, not because I want to look tough or nothing, but because there's so much sand and crap flying around. My hair and my jersey are blowing with that dirty wind. I got snot dripping from one nostril, and I don't care. "Stay put," Hotshot shouts. "Just keep that face!" And I'm wondering what on earth he's seeing through that camera.

Slow-Motioned and Blindsided

Something about playing football in a storm gets me all crazy in a good way. And playing at night with a storm is even better. But not tonight. There was this high, yowling wind pushing sand and dried grass and crumpled drink cups across the field. The bleachers was packed. Everybody was bundled up. It was so cold that the cheerleaders from both Claude and Lefors had sweatpants and sweatshirts on. It was like that wind was so mean that when a fellow tried running against it, never mind how fast he was going, he'd still think he wasn't hardly moving at all.

Anyway, no one scored during the first quarter. Us and the Leopards from Lefors just bumped around in that filthy weather not doing much of anything at all. In fact, I'd say the first quarter was downright dull. But then things started kicking in by the start of the second quarter. That's when we attempted a sweep to the right. I carried the ball just a couple of yards before getting clobbered in a cloud of dust. Then Sammy broke a pass pattern, fumbled the ball, and lost it. After that, the Leopards did a sneaky little play, gaining a few yards on us. And the whole time Coach Bud paced around nervously on the sidelines. Every now and then I heard him shout, "Come on!" Or, "Get after it!" And Effie from Lefors appeared like a statue on his side. He kept his arms folded. He chewed this huge hunk of gum in that big dumb face of his.

Finally, we got the ball again and tried a favorite play, but I gained only a couple of yards before them Leopards heaped over me. And each time I trudged on into the huddle, my face was dirtier and stickier with my own swelter, and the rest of the guys kept complaining on how them Leopards was tripping and grabbing and holding. I mean, more than twice Coach Bud jerked his head all angry as hell, yelling something at Effie like, "You're playing nasty, goddammit," though it mostly got swallowed in the wind.

And this is how it happened, or at least how I think it happened—

Lee handed me the ball, and I cradled it in my arms as I leaned into the line. Suddenly, I was past the line and gaining yards, even though that bitter breeze had me slowed to almost nothing. But I just knew I was in the clear. But I wasn't. BAM! I got nailed in the ribs by a cornerback. So I stumbled a little, broke the tackle, and shook him to the grass. I juked to the left and then cut to the right. Then BAM! Somebody from nowhere just laid into me like a ton of bricks. But I was driving ahead. My legs was still going. That second son of a bitch hung on my ass. He was doing his damnedest to topple me. But I was standing and dragging myself forward. Then this third Leopard bastard zoomed helmet first into my back. And soon as I was hitting the grass, this fuck of a fourth Leopard had to get into the act. I mean, I was already kissing the field, and here he came.

Next thing I knew, I was under a pile of Leopards. I could hear these whistles blowing. There was hands and legs and cleats sort of jabbing me everywhere. Someone had hold of my neck. Someone was just jostling my head around for some no-good reason. Jesus, I knew I was in trouble because my knee was twisting all weird. My right leg was cracking somewhere in that pile, and for a moment I didn't think that that sickening, crunching noise was coming from my body. Then I heard one of them bastards on top of me go, "That'll cool your ass, hotshit!" That's when all the white pain took over.

Once them Leopards was off me, I grabbed at my right knee. There I was just rolling around, groaning like a madman, and I spotted Lee and Sammy sort of floating above me with these frightened expressions. Then Coach Bud and Coach Slick was bending to where I was at. There was all these palms on my chest sort of rubbing my stomach. Coach Bud was going, "It's okay, son! Just hold on!" And that's about all I remember from the second quarter.

What I didn't know until after the game was that the minute those four Leopards squashed me, Coach Bud was charging across the field toward Effie. And Effie wasn't scared none either. He just held his ground, arms still folded, chewing that gum, and Coach Bud was bellowing every lousy word he could think of bellowing. Harvey told me Coach Bud was calling Effie a motherfucker and a cocksucker and a two-bit donkeydick. So Effie puckered his lips and gobbed that gum at Coach Bud. Harvey said Coach Bud got his fists raised and everything, but Slick and T.K. Maitland and some Lefors players sort of stopped any punches from getting thrown. Harvey said that once everyone got settled some, Effie just started pacing the sidelines with the grin of a creep.

During halftime, I found myself in Coach Bud's office. I was still in full uniform, all sweaty and beaten. Coach Bud and Slick stood behind me. Slick had his hands on my shoulders. They had me all slumped in one of them metal folding chairs. My right leg was propped on the edge of Coach Bud's desk. Doc was there too, and his fingers was dancing all over that leg of mine.

From the locker room I heard Sammy go, "How'd he get to him, man? How'd he get there?"

And Harvey went, "The play was over! It was over! He came in on a late whistle! He's a dead man! He's dead! If I can't get him tonight, I'll go to Lefors and cut his fucking throat! He's dead!"

Then a bunch of other guys started agreeing with Harvey, and Coach Bud hollered, "Keep it down in there! Just shut up!"

Then Doc had them fingers on my kneecap. He sort of rotated it, and that white pain shot all through me. My face got all screwy. I jerked my leg some, and Doc said, "Can't tell—hard to tell—"

And Coach Bud went, "Shit! Shit!" All of a sudden, he was crossing the room. Then he faced the wall behind his desk for a long time. Then he slammed that wall with open palms. Just

WHAP WHAP! And the whole damn office echoed with them slaps.

"It's okay, Coach," I said. "I can go—" and I don't know why I hauled off and told him that. I mean, there I was dying and all. But I was mad too. I wanted to get back on the field and do some business on them Leopards. To be honest, I had my mind set to find that fellow who went, "That'll cool your ass," and just pummel his mouth into nothing.

Coach Bud glanced at Doc. "Doc—?"

So Doc lifted his boney shoulders, bouncing that wild hair of his. "I suppose it's up to him."

Then Coach Bud came from that wall and squatted next to me. "We got a whole half left, son," he was saying. "How about it?"

And I felt Slick's hands kind of tense on my shoulders, and I wasn't sure if he was wanting me to play or not. "I can go," I said.

But Coach Bud didn't put me in until the fourth quarter. I spent most of the third quarter just walking along the sideline, sort of working out that knee. By the fourth, we was up on Lefors by seven points, and old Effie's face didn't seem so glad at the sight of me going into the game. He'd got a whole new stick of gum in his mouth. I bet he was chewing faster and faster when I took the ball, leaned forward, and ran some ten yards before being thrown to the ground by a pair of scrawny tacklers who got lucky.

Then I limped on into the huddle, my teeth gritting against the pain, but I was okay. The wind and dirt got pushing harder by the time I jogged that ball into the end zone. With something like two minutes left on the clock, we just toyed around with the Leopards until the game was done.

Not such a great win, but just seeing Coach Bud shaking his head at me with this look of admiration or something, and old Effie kicking at the grass on the sideline, his jaw smack smack smacking like nuts, got me eased inside. Then everyone came pouring from the bleachers onto the field. I had the whole of Claude ringed in around me. Pug and Stump and Junie and Bob and the entire rest of them was there. People was pounding on my back and stuff. And Hanna had her arms around me. It was like the end of a movie where the hero has won the big game and all his family and friends and everyone is there all weepy and clapping. I mean, someone would've thought I just beat cancer and won the Super Bowl.

And then I was sitting in front of Coach Bud's desk with my elbows on my legs. Showered clean. My hair still damp. All I had on was my shorts, and my right knee throbbed like a monster. Coach Bud and Doc was looking down at me. Coach Bud wore a worried, kind of anxious expression. Doc didn't have no expression at all. He was just blank. He pointed at my bad knee and went, "Soak her good over the weekend, son. Go easy on it till the swelling is gone. You call me tomorrow if it's really hurting you. We'll get you some medication."

"Thanks, Doc," I said.

Doc patted my wet head. Then he nodded at Coach Bud, who nodded in return. And nobody was saying a thing. Then Doc took his faded bag and left the office. Soon as the door shut, Coach Bud went, "You sleep on it. It'll feel better."

"It'll be okay," I said, trying to keep my face from giving away the pain.

"That was a hell of a game. You know it?"

But I wasn't so sure that I did know that, so I just shrugged instead.

"It'll go down as one of the best I've ever seen—anywhere! I want you to know that."

I kind of made my lips into a smile, but it wasn't sincere. I felt worn. My nose was all clogged. I wasn't in the mood for talk.

"We whipped them! Right into the dirt! Listen, son, before I let you go—I want you to know—I—I didn't mean to jump on you about that Newhouse call—I just want—well—what's best for us. You understand, don't you?"

"Sure," I said, "I understand." But the funny thing was, I couldn't stand Coach Bud at that moment. I don't know why.

Maybe it had something to do with the fact that I ain't feeling so hot, or that I'm just tired and droopy. I don't know.

So now I'm all alone in the locker room. I pull my T-shirt over my head, then I reach into my locker and get my letter jacket and put it on. Right away my hands go into those pockets, and my left hand finds my lucky charm. I take it out and hold it in my palm, and just seeing its little rhinestones shining makes my stomach do back-flips. And for some reason, just as I'm staring at Ramona's hairclip, I go, "Thanks," though I got no idea in the world why I said that. I really don't.

95 Points

It's like fall took a break today. I was by the front yard on this clear, sort of Indian summer of a Saturday, just throwing Nerf football passes to Joel, when I spotted that boxy red Yugo car easing along the road toward the house. Actually, because my knee still ain't right from last night, I was kind of sitting on the porch steps while Joel was out in the yard. I'd spiral a nice pass, nothing complicated, arching that pink ball under the bluest sky, then Joel would shoot all over the place trying to catch it; he'd get nervous and excited at once. His legs got goofy, like he had to pee real bad and couldn't stand still. He'd have one hand shielding his eyes some from the sun, and at least twice, because he'd got blinded by the glare, that Nerf bounced right off his T-shirt and rolled on the ground.

So along came Mr. Lockhart's Yugo, which he's pretty proud of. When he bought that thing last year almost everyone in town had something to say about it. T. K. Maitland called it "a turd of a car," and Coach Bud kept joking on how Mr. Lockhart had gone all the way to Amarillo one afternoon to eat at McDonald's and came home with a McCar Happy Meal. Even Sammy, who don't have a truck or a car or nothing, said, "I'd rather drive a wheelchair than be caught in that thing." As for me, I don't know, it's just a car. But it's sort of cute.

Anyway, that Yugo got halfway up the drive before stopping. And right as I was about to throw the Nerf, the horn honked a couple of times. That's when I got a bit shaky with the idea that Mr. Lockhart had come all this way for some reason. I mean, I was amazed he even knew where I lived. Then I got to worrying about

122

Hanna, because she's on a weekend UIL competition in Abilene. I thought something bad might have happened, like maybe the school bus had wrecked or got hit by a train. Or maybe he was about to jump my ass for getting rough on his daughter that night in my truck, though I know Hanna wouldn't say a word about that.

So without really paying attention, I tossed the football at Joel, who was turned around from me and looking at the Yugo, and told him, "Hold on a second," though I don't think he heard what I said. When that Nerf bonked him in the back of the skull, he shouted out all surprised and annoyed, which would've made me laugh most other times.

Then I was limping away from the house, stepping through the brush to where that Yugo idled. I crossed on over to the driver's side, where the window was rolled down, and Mr. Lockhart was there with those damn pens and his glasses stuck in the breast pocket of his shirt. "Did I interrupt something?" he was saying, grinning at me like I was his long-lost brother or someone.

"Just messing with Joel," I told him.

"Why don't you take a little ride with me, Willy."

So I shrugged. "Okay," I said, except I didn't say it right away. I just kind of paused and glanced to where Joel was watching with that Nerf ball by his shoes, then I glanced to Mr. Lockhart, who was nodding his head at me for some dumbass reason. Then I went, "Okay."

Next thing I knew, we was driving across this lonely, desolate stretch of bumpy road in the Caprock. We was in the hell of nowhere. Mr. Lockhart had the radio tuned to some Amarillo country station, and every now and then he'd drum his fingers on the steering wheel. The whole time he just rambled about how nice today is, how great the game was last night, how I done Claude C.S.D. good. Then he asked about my knee. He asked if I had a problem walking. He wanted to know if it hurt to run.

To be truthful, the entire conversation creeped me and then some, especially the way he kept acting friendly and grinny. I mean, I imagined him pulling over suddenly. I saw him ordering me to get out and telling me I got three seconds to run for my life. And before I ever realized what happened—BLAM! Then I'd be laying in my own blood and crap, just squirming like a wounded jackrabbit in scrub brush, and Mr. Lockhart would be grinning that grin above me with a 9mm or something in hand, going, "You had to go and get rough on Hanna," or, "Too bad it had to end this way, son, but you had it coming."

Anyway, Mr. Lockhart just went on yapping and dancing his fingers to Rosanne Cash and being my buddy, then from the blue he goes, "It's all a phase," which was a weird thing to haul off and say for no reason. I mean, he'd been talking about how high school pride pulled a small community together, then he jumped in with, "What it is is a phase—just a phase this high school is, and when kids get through it, then their whole lives start all over again. It's different after this. You ever think on that, Willy?"

"I guess not much," I said.

"I been an educator for some twenty years, and I guess I know better than anybody—when you leave high school, you're leaving one world behind and going into the next—and if you try to mix them, it just won't work. You know what I'm saying?"

"No, sir," I told him, "I guess I don't."

That was when I spotted the speech coming. His voice changed. The Yugo slowed a bit. His brow got pinched. He got all serious and thoughtful. He'd appeared just like that this morning, right before our English teacher, Mrs. Christian, and Hanna and Jackie Maitland and these two freshman twin sisters called Tanya and Toni McCarthy, as well as this Mexican kid named Juan Garcia, who's a sophomore and who doesn't play football and who's real quiet on account of the fact that he stutters something awful, boarded that school bus for Abilene.

Not a whole bunch of folks showed up at the school to see Hanna and them leave for the UIL competitions, but I made it, as did T.K. Maitland and Mrs. Maitland and Mr. Lockhart and Mrs. Lockhart. But Juan's parents didn't come, and only Tanya and Toni's mother was there for them. Still, everyone acted nice about being bothered so early in the morning. Someone brought coffee and hot chocolate and these donuts with a great cream filling. Most of the parents and everyone else stood together in the parking lot, visiting with each other, so I managed to get Hanna away for a moment.

We walked around behind the bus so no one could see us. I was still sort of guilty for having gotten all wild with her in my truck. But Hanna seemed fine. She was pretty happy about taking part in the Ready Writing competition, and Mrs. Christian felt fairly certain that Hanna would come home with a ton of ribbons. "You'll be the best one there," I told her.

"I hope so."

Then there was this silence. And I was staring right at her, but her eyes just fell on something past me, so I said, "Hey, I— I'm really sorry about—you know—"

Then her eyes kind of locked on my eyes, and right as she was about to open her mouth, Mr. Lockhart shouted, "All right, everyone listen."

In a flash we was stepping from behind that bus. Mr. Lockhart stood in front of everyone, so Hanna and I sort of joined the crowd. That was when I noticed that face of his, all pinched and severe. He was saying, "It's about time for these kids to get on the road, but I want everyone to know that this is a big day for Claude. We're really proud of all the students going to Abilene today. To get to regional in UIL is an honor for the students and for the school. They're the best in Ready Writing, Spelling, and Illustrated Talks. Now, maybe these students don't get the crowds or attention they should, but it's very important and it's an honor. We wish them all our best today, and we know they'll bring credit to Claude. We're with them a hundred percent." Then Mr. Lockhart gave a nod at the students, and there was a tinkle of applause from the parents and me. Then Mr. Lockhart went, "The bus will return at around ten tonight, so you parents need to be here to get your kids. All right, load up!"

So Hanna gave me this quick kiss on the cheek, which was a dangerous thing to do in front of her dad. Then I said, "Let me know how it goes."

And once Hanna and the rest was on the bus, T.K. came over to me and went, "How's that leg doing?" Then he threw a big arm across my shoulders. He was kind of hugging me, sort of patting my back, and just as that bus was pulling away, I spotted Jackie's face watching us. And it got me all sad inside for some reason, because T.K. was just going on and on, saying, "You done great last night," and Jackie was gazing from his seat without any real expression. And T.K. didn't wave or nothing as that bus left.

Another thing was, as I watched all them UILers get on that bus, I kind of wished I was going with them. I mean, Mrs. Christian told me I could write okay, so I figure I could've gone to regional in Ready Writing like Hanna. And if it weren't for football and everything, I'd probably have tried to compete in the UIL. So soon as I got home, I dug through my old English notebooks. I mean, some of the stuff I've written down ain't bad.

Like last year, Mrs. Christian told us all to keep a journal, and every night we had to write something in it for a grade. Of all the things I wrote, there's at least a few I like.

September 9

A TERRIBLE DAY

A terrible day can be very bad. You may wake up on the wrong side of the bed, and then you have a terrible day. Not getting enough sleep can cause a bad day too. I know, because I have had bad days before.

September 17

COLDNESS

Staying warm when it's cold is very tough. You can get by a fire to stay warm, but if you move away from it you will get cold again. You can stay warm with a blanket, or even warm with an electric blanket. You can stay warm by wearing a lot of clothing, such as thermal underwear. If your brother don't bug you much, you both can just share a bed and stay warm together. A good way to stay warm when it's cold is not to go outside. You may also stay warm by putting on coats. To keep your hands warm just rub them together or wear gloves. To keep your head warm, you can wear a hat.

October 3

LITTLE KIDS

Little kids are a big pain. Little kids are always griping or complaining about something. If they don't get their way they start crying and that would annoy anyone. And little kids always get their way while the older brothers get in trouble for what they do. But little kids can be all right sometimes. Like when they are asleep. I like just born kids better than I do older ones. But the just born kids don't always smell that good either. And little kids are always getting into some kind of trouble. They don't understand how to dress either. They sometimes make a ton of noise too, especially where there is a whole bunch together. They also have a hard time using the bathroom. That is why little kids are a big pain.

November 15

CIGARETTES

Cigarettes are seen all over the world these days. Cigarettes can become a habit, and an expensive one at that. Cigarettes are about four inches long, and some are different than that. Some cost about a $1.25 a package. So if you are a heavy smoker, it can become very expensive. Cigarettes are also bad for your health. It could cause death from smoking. They also have a very bad odor and stink. What's worse is when a parent smokes cigarettes, and some guy and his brother watch TV and almost choke from all the smoking their mom and her friends are doing.

I was stretched out on my bed with that ratty notebook, sort of admiring some of my writing, when I got to thinking on how I should write this book about me. Not so much the real story, something more like the movies or something. I'd have me and there'd be Hanna and everyone. But I'd change all the names so no one would sue me or nothing. Then I thought about how I know football, and how that might make a good book. I went about creating titles. I think I must have jotted twenty or thirty titles this morning. My two favorites are *On the Line* and *End Zone.*

Then I started figuring on how I'd make a book about this college football star who falls in love with some older woman, except the older woman wouldn't be called Ramona or any such name. I thought of calling her Cindy. And I thought I'd call the guy Tom. Cindy and Tom. Then there'd be a really rotten fellow, who'd be named something like Arnold or Crispin. And this Arnold or Crispin would be very rich and try to take Cindy from Tom. I don't know how it'd all come together, because just about the time I was beginning work on the details, Joel came into our bedroom and asked if I wanted to throw the Nerf around.

And while I was on that porch giving Joel passes, I realized Tom needed a younger brother. This younger brother would be like Tom's sidekick, and the two of them would make these plans to deal with Arnold or Crispin. But the brother would be crippled on account of the fact that he'd been injured in the factory Arnold or Crispin's father owned. I haven't got a name for the brother yet.

Then Mr. Lockhart drove up, and the funny thing was, as I rode along in that Yugo with him, my mind kept floating to my book. I'd have Mr. Lockhart in it for sure, except he'd be called Waymore or someone like that. He'd be Arnold or Crispin's father, an oilman from Amarillo, and he'd be the last bad guy Tom took care of at the very end. Of course, all them thoughts disappeared when Mr. Lockhart started in on his speech.

"What I'm saying, Willy," he was telling me, "is that me and Mother have been planning for Hanna since she was a baby. Making real careful plans. When she graduates, she's going to Texas Tech, and she's going to meet new people. She's going to do new things. She's going to get an education that's the best Texas can offer, and as far as I'm concerned, that's the best in the country. She's going to teach—maybe high school at first, but later at the university level."

Then he got that Yugo stopped in the center of that nowhere road. He clicked the radio off. He twisted around with this hard face, and his voice took on a kind of tough tone: "She's not going to quit college because she thinks she's missing out on something somewhere else—something that amounts to nothing more than this high school thing! Nosir! She's not going to be miserable or think about getting married or anything else for a long time! I don't want anybody trailing around after her trying to change her mind! I guess it's just better for you to know this right here and now!"

And when I went, "You're saying you don't want me seeing Hanna anymore," he sort of forced a smile.

"Aw, I'm not a mean man and you know that," he said. "You two are going to see each other finish the year. No stopping that. No reason to, I guess. When you two graduate, then you figure out what you're going to do, and don't follow after Hanna anymore, okay? She's going to be going in a different direction. You know what I'm saying?"

But I didn't nod or nothing. I just turned my head and studied that dirty red road. I don't know if my face showed hurt or anger or just blankness. But what I was thinking was that when Tom finally does get around to taking care of Waymore, he's going to kill him real slow, real painful. He's going to stick that oilman stomach first on this huge razor, which will be about as wide and long as a playground slide. Then he's going to send old Waymore down that razor into a pool of peroxide. When they make the movie of my book, people will be clapping at that part.

Anyway, the trip home took forever. Mr. Lockhart didn't say a word. Neither did I. There wasn't music this time around either, just that Yugo growling through the Caprock. The truth is, I might be a little more torn about this if it wasn't for Ramona. I mean, it ain't Hanna I'm thinking about at night no more. It ain't nobody but Ramona. I guess I should feel bad about that, but I don't. I still love Hanna and all. But I mean, if it weren't for Ramona hiding in my head, I might've whapped old Waylon for saying what he said.

When Mr. Lockhart got to our house, just as I was about to climb from his car, he went, "I suppose for everybody's benefit, this should stay between you and me. You know what I'm saying?"

"We'll see," I said, though I didn't figure I was going to tell anyone. Then I stood in the drive and slammed that door, and my knee throbbed something terrible when I did that. And as Mr. Lockhart was backing away, Joel came over to me with the Nerf, saying, "You want to pass some more, Willy?"

"Not now," I said. "Maybe later."

Then I limped on into the house, and that's where I am now. I'm on my bed with my junior English notebook. And anyway, I'm recalling something about Mr. Lockhart that gets me steamed. There ain't much to it, but it sort of points out the kind of man he is, which in my opinion is sneaky. He's a sneaky man. A fellow has no idea what's going on in that brain of his, though I imagine it's fairly bent around and black. It's like he gets talking like he's a preacher sometimes, all proper and better than everyone, but inside he's got Hitler going, "Exterminate!"

And what I'm remembering is how one Sunday last year, I stayed the night at Lee's house to study for this test in Mr. Lockhart's first-period History class—even though he's the principal and all, he still teaches a class every so often. So me and Lee studied all night about the Battle of the Atlantic and Rommel's attempt to outflank the First Army and all that stuff that went on at the Anzio Beachhead. And I swear we thought we was going to ace that test.

But what happened was we stirred late. It's not that the alarm didn't buzz or nothing. It did. But we was both too lazy to get moving from Lee's bed. Then we had to chomp breakfast, because Lee's mom fried a big mess of pork chops. She'd made biscuits too. Then we had to shower and everything. I mean, we weren't that late to school, maybe fifteen minutes or so, but by the time we arrived at Mr. Lockhart's class, the test was already going on. So Mr. Lockhart made us wait in the hall until everyone had finished. That's when me and Lee figured our little plan. Lee said we should just explain to Mr. Lockhart that we got a flat tire on the way to school. "How could he punish us for that?"

"He can't."

So that's what we told him. And he was fairly nice about it too. "Don't sweat it, boys," he said. "Just stop by my office after school and I'll give you a makeup exam." And that's what we did. We stopped by his office after school, and he told me to take a seat behind Busy Bess' desk. So I did. Then he had Lee go sit in a big utility closet. Then Mr. Lockhart went into his office and came back out with the tests. He put mine in front of me, saying, "Good luck." Then he went over to where Lee was, handed him the test, went, "Good luck," and shut that utility closet door.

But there was only two questions on that test. The first one was: For 5 points, what was Britain's chief trouble in home waters?

I wrote that answer right away. E-boats.

The second question read: For 95 points, which tire?

See what I'm talking about? Sneaky. The whole damn day he was looking forward to nailing me and Lee. And it didn't matter at all that we busted our nuts studying for the real test. It made no difference. Even if we'd gotten a flat, he'd still think we was lying. I call that evil. That's what I'm talking about. And if it weren't for Ramona giving me this kiss in my memory, and John Wayne sort of bubbling from my throat and telling me, "Every low-down and dirty dog gets his," I'd probably be crazy right now.

Southern Comforts
and Precious Moments

I'd have made the climb, but I can't imagine my knee allowing it, so me and Sammy are perched in the tall grass below the water tower instead. It's Sunday night. We're sharing a pint of Southern Comfort I stole from the glove box of Stump's truck. It's so bright outside that I can spot the colors on the water tower from the ground.

"Don't matter if Lilah don't want to see me no more," Sammy says. "It don't matter," though I suspect it does.

I go, "We don't need them. You don't need Lilah. I don't need Hanna. It ain't the end of the world or nothing, right?"

"That's right, Willy. You said a mouthful."

And it's a fine night. The moon is full, kind of yellow and close to the earth. I blow steam between my lips. From my nose to toes, my body is warm from the hooch.

Sammy leans his head against me, so I ruffle his twisty hair, and he goes, "You ever cry?"

"Not so much no more. I don't remember when I last did."

"Me neither."

"You feel like crying?"

"No. You?"

"No."

"That's all right too."

Sometimes me and Sammy get blue at the same moments. Sometimes it's like we're connected or something. He'll just appear at my place on his Huffy bicycle. He'll knock on my bedroom window at night, or on the front door at day, going, "Say, you want to get the hell out of here?" Or it'll be me making the two-mile drive to his place and we'll go somewhere and mope.

The thing is, most folks think it's okay to associate with a black at school or on the team, or if a guy has a mess of blacks working for him, but just hanging out with one for no good reason other than friendship, well, people lift an eyebrow or two about that. Of course, I've known Sammy since Mom and Dad moved me and Joel to Claude. He was the first pal I made here, so I don't treat him like I'm supposed to. I don't treat him as a black or nothing. He's just Sammy. That's how Lee sees him too. And for that matter, me and Lee are more than just two white guys to Sammy.

If ever there was somebody to just get blue with, it'd be Sammy, because he's got a way of cheering a guy. Maybe it's on account of the fact that he's so damn funny. I mean, there we'll be, butts on some hill outside of Claude, sort of sad about life and stuff. We'll be all thoughtful and deep with our arms on our knees. Crickets might be squeaking, and we'll be gazing over this long view of prairie and farmland that stretches from Claude to the Caprock. So I'll say something like, "What's going to happen to us, Sammy?"

And he'll go, "We'll get out of here, man. One way or another, we'll get out of here." Then he'll suddenly say, "This carrot tastes pithy," but he won't be eating a carrot or anything.

So I'll go, "Yeah, it's pithy 'cause I pithed on it," and that'll somehow get us in a lighter mood. That's kind of our little joke when we're down.

To be honest, I kind of worry about Sammy. It's not like he's got scouts checking him out. He don't got money for college, and he ain't saving any money from his weekend work with T.K. Truthfully, he's a lot different than his older brother Eric, who busted his ass in high school, and got a track scholarship to UT. Eric was good in sports, except he didn't make them his life. It's like Eric had his mind on the future, but Sammy don't think that way at all. In fact, the last person in the world he'd want to be like is Eric. The two never got along in the past, and they don't get along now. I mean, he's tried so hard to be the opposite of his brother that he may just end up staying in Claude. He'll probably wrangle for T.K. forever, except I'd hate that to happen. Of course, it ain't my place to tell him what I think he should do. He never asks me anyway. But what kind of friend would I be if I didn't worry about him some?

Sammy's mother calls me Willyhead. I got no idea why I'm Willyhead, but she's named me that as long as I can remember. Her name is Tamla. She works at the courthouse, though I don't know what it is she does there. Sammy's father left after he was born, so Tamla just buckled up and took care of business.

She bought a house not too far from where I live, sort of far and lonely from Claude. It was a real mess with just barely two bedrooms and a living room and a bathroom and a kitchen. The floorboards was all bowed and wobbly in spots. The green carpet just sort of dipped here and there. When they moved in, that place didn't even own front or back doors. It didn't even have proper plumbing because the pipes had rusted into nothing. Then her and Sammy and Eric set about fixing that heap on the weekends. For about two years they patched on it. The three of them shingled the entire roof from lumber scraps and stuff, and pretty soon they had themselves an honest home. Really, I don't know many folks who'd go out of their way to repair some wreck of a dump like that.

The thing about Tamla is that she's always sweet to me. "Guess you're going to have to stay for supper, Willyhead," she'll say. Or, "How come more of you ain't rubbed off on Sammy, Willyhead?" which gets me and Sammy going really good. Every Christmas she's got something for me. Last year it was socks. The year before that it was socks.

Used to be, when I'd spend the night over at Sammy's, Tamla would stay up late with us and play records. She has all these great old albums. Lots of stuff I've never heard of. "Oh, the pain in my heart," she'd go, smiling wide at me and Sammy, then that stereo needle would come down on some scratchy music, like James Brown or Otis Redding. Crazy things like that. Can't say I love the funk or anything, but it's okay. Listening to "Motor Booty Affair" or "Funkentelechy vs. the Placebo Syndrome" is fine too, as long as I can just sit on that holey couch and watch Tamla, in the middle of that living room, dancing with herself or Sammy or Eric, singing to those P-funk songs out here in the sticks.

Something else about Tamla that comes to mind. She collects these Precious Moments figurines, which are kind of strange and silly. She's got maybe a hundred of them. She says they're worth a lot of money now, though I don't know why anyone in the world would want one. Some of these Precious Moments are angels, but most others are just a boy and a girl. Sometimes it's a boy and a girl together with this kitten and puppy. They're all white and pasty looking on account of they're made of porcelain or something. But what bugs me most about those Precious Moments is their eyes, which are huge and round, almost taking over their entire heads, which ain't normal at all. It's like they're aliens or some preborn kids or worse. Their heads are too damn big for their bodies too, and they got these grins that are supposed to be cute. I mean, Jesus, if some actual kids appeared like that in real life, people would tear off in the opposite direction screaming. People wouldn't think they was cute at all. Not for a second, believe me.

Even Eric thinks them Precious Moments are weird, except he ain't Eric no more. When he came home to visit last summer from Austin, he was Amilcar. He had his hair in these dreadlock things. He wore a knit skullcap with all these colorful patterns and designs. I swear to God, I ain't ever seen someone change so fast in my life. Eric used to be sort of loud and fun to be with, but Amilcar has a soft tone and is intense. Eric ate bacon and pork chops for breakfast like a madman, but Amilcar doesn't. That kind of stuff about drives Sammy nuts. He refuses to call Eric anything but Eric, and that pisses Amilcar off to no end. Once Sammy told

Eric on the phone, "Just leave old Amilcar in Austin," but he wasn't kidding. That's just how those two are, always arguing over the littlest of things.

Anyway, while we was all sitting in the living room listening to this 45 by a bunch known as the Ohio Players, Eric asked Tamla, "Mama, why does a beautiful black woman like yourself trouble collecting a bunch of ugly, spooky-faced white children? Don't you see the hypocrisy in that? Ever seen a black Precious Moment? Of course not."

But Tamla just shrugged, going, "It's me owning the white kids, Amilcar, not the other way around," which I thought was pretty funny.

That's the thing I don't like about Eric now. Before he was Amilcar, him and I could shoot the shit about the Dallas Cowboys or the Bulls or even the Oilers. But now all that stuff doesn't interest him. Hell, he hardly even says "Hi" to me when I see him these days. I guess he's got his brain on all kinds of new things, which is good, but I sure do understand how he'd get on Sammy's nerves.

Last summer, for example, Tamla had cooked us a pile of greens and mashed potatoes and some fried catfish, so I just tried to make conversation over that meal by asking Eric, "You been keeping up with the Cowboys at UT?"

"No," he said, but in an abrupt kind of manner.

So I went, "How about the Longhorns?"

And Eric didn't say nothing. He just shook his head. He kept his face aimed all sullen at his plate. I mean, I thought he was angry or something.

Then Sammy said, "Don't mind him, Willy. People like us are just ignorant country butts."

And Tamla piped in with, "Ain't nobody here thinks nobody is stupid here."

So Eric just dropped his fork on his plate. He tossed his napkin on the table, scooted from his seat, and walked from the kitchen without even saying, "Excuse me." Like I've mentioned, it's all right if someone wants to change and all, but they don't have to be an asshole when they do it.

Now the pint is empty.

Sammy goes, "You ever think about dying?"

"Not much. Sometimes."

"I do. Almost every day."

"That ain't good."

"I know."

"Hey, how's that carrot tasting?"

"Pithy as hell, man."

Sammy chunks that Southern Comfort bottle. It bursts into a million bits across the chain-link fence surrounding us.

Bodies Above Ground

It was Sammy who urged me to pick up Hanna. It was also his idea to head on over to Clover Hill. Personally, there's something a little wrong in my mind about getting all horny with a girl in a place meant for dead folks, but Sammy's right about it being the last place in the world people go searching for someone alive. I mean, if it weren't for the fact that he's with Jamie Lynn, who's this white girl from Conway, I don't think he'd have bothered with the cemetery.

Most guys in Claude know of Jamie Lynn on account of the fact that she makes no bones about liking sex. Let's just say she makes the rounds. "Plain trash," is how Hanna sees her. "She'd screw her own father if she knew who he was," except I don't know if that's so true. The thing is, Sammy got to feeling pretty sorry for himself when Lilah broke up with him last Friday. So he phoned Jamie Lynn, asked what she was doing, and two hours later she'd hitchhiked from Conway to Claude, which ain't even that far to begin with.

Here it is not being summer and all, but Jamie Lynn's wearing stringy denim shorts and a purple tank top. Her skin is pale and ghosty; it's almost as if she ain't ever been under the sun in her life. That bloody red lipstick she's got smudged around her lips makes me think of some circus clown, like Bozo or somebody, or the Joker in Batman. And those shorts are cut so high that her ass peeks from the bottoms like half-moons. Don't forget that her hair is bunched and sprayed and swirled to where it appears like she's got a satellite dish above her forehead. Hanna says Jamie Lynn's hair is like that to catch all the crap that goes over her head, which might be the case. Either way, she ain't what someone might call bright. She's not even close to stupid. She's kind of pitiful in my opinion. When she saw Sammy, after coming all those miles to be with him, she went, "Oh, yeah, I remember you." Hanna almost went nuts when I told her that.

So now Hanna and I are stretched together on the grassy mound of a grave belonging to *Helmut Millard, Our Beloved Father, 1896–1948,* and Sammy and Jamie Lynn are off on their own. It's a real pleasant evening, sort of warm and unseasonable, though not warm enough for a guy to be without his letter jacket. I'm flat on my back. Hanna is on an elbow and kissing down on me. Then her mouth lifts from my mouth. Her fingers squeeze gently between my legs. Next thing I know, I'm brushing her hand away from my crotch.

"I was only checking if it was hard," she says, sounding all hurt.

"It's not."

So she goes, "What's wrong?"

"Nothing," I say.

"Something is—why aren't you talking to me?"

"I am. I guess I just don't have much to say—"

Then her voice gets whiny. "Oh, my gosh," she jokes, "Willy Keeler doesn't have something to say! Let me call the papers! Stop the presses!"

Then I go, "Why are you in such a good mood?"

And she says, "I don't know. Do I need a reason?"

I shrug.

"I mean, I was second in Ready Writing—I'm sure now, I'm going to be valedictorian and not Patsy—and I've got you! I don't know why I'm in a good mood. Anyway, I should be mad at you for not coming to meet the bus the other night."

"My knee was killing me."

"That's why you're down, ain't it?"

"I ain't down."

The truth is, I'm happier than I've been in memory. But it's not something I can tell her. Because if I told her I was happy, I'd have to lie about why. And I don't want to do that to her. Not yet. It's like I got this secret that's so wonderful, sort of special in a way, that if I haul off and let anyone know, it'd be ruined in a flash.

Anyway, how could I explain being in bed the other night. My head still spinning some from the bourbon I'd shared with Sammy. I hadn't even bothered to crawl under the covers, so I was just lying there in my shorts. I had a foot on the carpet to keep me from getting too dizzy. And everything was silent, except for the racket of the old alarm clock tick tick ticking on my dresser. I couldn't sleep worth shit.

Then before I knew it, I'd swung my legs to the floor, heaved myself up, and kind of winced at the pain coming from my knee. So there I was in darkness, stepping over to the chair beside my dresser. I took my Wranglers and started to pull them on. Then I grabbed my T-shirt. And I was doing all this as noiseless as possible, because I didn't want to wake Joel.

Next thing I recall, I was zooming along 287 in my truck. By then my insides had got all twisty. My palms was sweaty. I had that rhinestone hairclip in my pocket, sort of stabbing into my leg, and all I could think about was how I shouldn't have stole it to begin with.

I paced over that ratty hotel carpet for I don't know how long. I wasn't even sure if I had the room number remembered right. All I kept wondering was, "What the hell are you going to say, Willy?" Then I finally got the nerve, even though I was edgy as hell. I placed myself smack in front of 219, sort of stared at the splintery crack cutting straight down the center of the door. I knocked twice with my knuckles, but very gentle. Then I kind of leaned into that door hoping to catch something, but all I heard was the gurgle of water pipes in the walls around me. That's when I got sort of worried that I'd bust on through that crack, because my shoulder was pressing into the wood pretty hard, so I stepped away and knocked once more. I guess I waited another minute or so after that, then I figured Ramona wasn't home. And right as I turned to leave, that door opened kind of careful and squeaky.

I swear Ramona was beautiful in my mind, but nothing in the world prepared me for the sight of her then. She had on sweatpants and a blue T-shirt. She was barefoot. Her hair was sort of hanging wild around her head. And what's funny is that I kept imagining her with that bumped and bruised face, so to see her without all that damage surprised me to no end. I mean, if I'd thought she was gorgeous as a prizefighter, she was nearly a million times more attractive then. I guess I must've looked fairly shocked or something, because soon as she saw my expression she went, "Is Pug all right?"

"Oh, yeah," I mumbled, "yeah." Then I just couldn't put any more words in my mouth. I became a total idiot, and Ramona didn't appear too glad at the sight of me.

"Why are you here?"

I shook my head. "I just wanted—I—" then my head bowed toward my boots.

"I guess I know what you want," she said.

That about sent me running. I glanced up and saw her face showing something like anger. "No—no—it ain't that at all. I just—"

"You been drinking?"

"A little is all."

Her expression softened some, which made me feel a whole lot better. She kind of nodded, then grinned a bit from the corner of her mouth. Then she moved on into her room, leaving that door wide open. And I didn't know what to do then. I didn't know if I was supposed to follow, or just stand in the hallway like a complete goof.

Ramona sat on the edge of her bed. I was sitting nearby in this wicker chair, watching as she reached for the telephone on the bedstand. She hit a one-digit number, and in no time she was talking to someone on the other end of the line. "If he calls," she was saying, "ring me—but nothing else tonight—huh?" Her brow got all scruffled at whatever the person on the other end was going on about. Then her eyes shot to me. "It ain't like that," she practically hollered. Then she just hung up without even going, "Goodbye."

I didn't say a word as she stretched out on that bed with this exhausted sigh. She sort of fluffed the pillow behind her head, then she went, "Are you going to just sit there and stare?"

"Sorry," I said, my cheeks growing hot, then I glanced at my hands in my lap.

"Don't have to be sorry, just don't stare."

"Okay," I said. And it seemed like forever we was there like that—me kind of studying the lines on my palms, but not really, while I knew her eyes was doing to me what she'd told me not to do to her. So I asked, "Are you happy," which made Ramona snort a laugh like a cough.

"Are you?"

I looked at her and noticed she was chewing at a fingernail. "I don't know," I said. "I guess not always."

"There you go," she said. Then she went, "Look, you're a nice boy, and I don't want to be rude, but I've had a long night, and I really don't know what it is you want."

"I just want to see you again, that's all. Just see you," and I felt real stupid for saying it like that. I guess I'd planned to be smoother, or cooler. I guess I imagined myself having this mature, French voice, going, "Ramona, you don't know how I've longed for you. To be near you. To touch you." All the same, what came from me seemed to work just fine, because she brought that finger she was munching on from her mouth. Then she gave me an honest smile; the kind of smile that goes, "I like you."

And when she went, "You're a strange boy," her voice was sort of easy, almost sweet. Then she said, "You got troubles, do you? Shouldn't you be home or anything? It's well after midnight."

"It don't matter."

"You're tired?"

"Yeah."

She patted the other side of the bed, saying, "Well, take off your boots and lie down awhile."

And that's exactly what I did. I yanked those boots from my feet like a psycho, then I walked around that bed and laid myself out beside her. Truthfully, I didn't have no nasty thoughts in mind. I just wanted to be near her. And I know she was feeling the same, because once I got settled in a comfortable way, she shifted a bit so her head came to rest on my shoulder. And the odor of her was like how a body gets after a shower, sort of scrubbed and soapy.

Pretty soon my eyes shut. Then I got all heavy. At that moment I felt kind of bad, because I knew there wasn't no way I was giving back that hairclip. Then I heard air escaping from Ramona's mouth, and I listened for a time as her breathing got deeper and deeper. And that's how I fell asleep, with that clean smell in my nose. I don't think I've ever slept so good in my life.

The sky has grown all dark on top, with blue and orange around the edges. I'm trying to spot these stars that Joel once showed me as being the Winter Triangle, except I don't think I'm looking where I'm supposed to. Hanna is leaning against old Helmut Millard's tombstone and going, "How come you keep saying it's up to Coach Bud? I mean, you could go to Tech with me—it's close to home—we'd be together—and what does it matter *where* you play football?" But all I can find are two or three white stars and this one flashing red star that might be an airplane. "And besides, I'd be a freshman and already dating a football player!"

"Don't bite me, girl," Sammy yells, and I can hear him and Jamie Lynn carrying on somewhere nearby.

And Jamie Lynn goes, "You're the craziest black boy I've ever known," and it strikes me odd how there's like three cemeteries in one here. The blacks, deposited in some of the weediest plots ever, are over beyond the mesquites at the back fence, and the Mexicans, which account for a lot of the newer graves, are on the other end near the gravel path by the side fence. The middle of this place is filled with all the rest of the Claude folks who ain't either black or Mexican, though Stump was saying how not too long ago the Catholics and the Baptists got put apart. I mean, everybody was busy praying to the same fellow on Sundays, but they couldn't bother to be dead next to each other. Go figure on that.

As far as I'm concerned, it's the Mexican graves I like the best, because there's usually a tiny picture of the person put on the tombstone, which is sort of neat and creepy at the same time. I guess it's only creepy because I never imagine the people buried under here as having faces, or as ever having been young or anything. Anyway, the Mexican graves always got fresh flowers on them, and there's this little grave in particular that always draws me. It's just some boy, born March 23, 1968, and died March 27, 1968, named only Tito. The tombstone has Our Precious Lamb carved in the granite below this small statue of a sleeping lamb, but there ain't no picture to be seen. Also, stuck and almost covered over in the yellow grass of that grave are these ancient toy soldiers that have been there forever. I mean, it's not like the kid ever got a chance to even play with those soldiers or anything.

"What you thinking?" Hanna says.

"Not a thing," I tell her.

Just then Sammy and Jamie Lynn come jogging by without giving us notice. They're giggling and acting silly like a pair of goons. Sammy's got dried grass all over his shirt, and Jamie Lynn's hair looks deflated in the moonlight. They get several yards away, then disappear behind some bushes by the front gate. Jamie Lynn is bellowing, but not in a bad way, going, "Stop it! Stop it!"

And Sammy is saying, "Don't you dare! Don't you even do it—"

Hanna shakes her head all disgusted. "She's trash. I can't believe even Sammy would be with her."

"Even Sammy," I say.

Hanna flushes. "Well, I didn't mean—" Then she bends and

I let her kiss me. I close my eyes and taste her spit, all thick and slippery, sort of like how drool gets after a guy drinks a glass of milk. Our tongues dance around some. I bring my arms around her waist, but it ain't her I'm holding. And it's real quiet now. I can't hear Sammy or Jamie Lynn. I can't hear nothing except the slobbery squish our mouths are making.

Return of
the Great American Death Car

Mom's face got all red like it does when she gets crazy. She was going, "Go live with the bastard! I don't give a shit! You and Joel both!" I swear I wanted to just grab that Elvis Commemorative Gold-Plated Dish from its place on the wall and smash it right in front of her. That'd have been something. I'd have jumped smack-dab on the King, busting him into nothing more than painted chunks on the living room carpet. I really should've done that, except now I'm on the water tower and I'm not nearly as mad as then. Anyway, there's no need to insult the King or anything. It ain't his fault. Not that none of it is mine or Joel's fault either.

I mean, there we was taking a late-afternoon walk. I was sort of working out my knee, getting it in shape before Friday. And we was a mile or so from the house, kind of stepping through scrub on the shoulder of this nowhere road. Joel was explaining to me about a story he'd found in the library. He was saying how there was this guy who'd got it in his head to swim across all the swimming pools in his neighborhood to get home. And that guy would just swim across one pool and then go to the next pool and do it again. But the clinker was, once he got to his house, the doors was locked and the place was empty. "Pretty sad, huh?" Joel said.

And I went, "Yeah," though I didn't get what was so sad about it. The guy was obviously dumb or something. Why else would he be doing that when there's probably sidewalks and everything? Jesus, I figure he just ended up at the wrong house, but was too stupid to realize it.

Joel said, "Sometimes I'll just take any book from the shelf at the library and start reading it. It's kind of surprising like that. You never know what you'll find."

And I was just about to tell him that I thought that was a good idea, because being surprised is a whole lot better than knowing what boring book *has* to get read for some class, when I spotted a car bumping our way real fast. It was spinning dirt all over the place, flying toward us like the end of the world was chasing it. Me and Joel just sort of stopped in our steps. "Who is it?" he asked, sounding a bit spooked.

"I don't know," I said, because the dust getting thrown around that car sort of made it impossible to spot anything but the shine of the grill. Then as it got closer, as I started making out the red hood, I had me an idea who it might be. And when I realized that car could be nothing else except a Ford Mustang, I told Joel, "It's Dad."

"You sure?" Joel said, kind of pressing into me, his eyes fixed on that Mustang's approach.

"I ain't sure." And I knew what must've been going on inside Joel's head—he about shoved a hole through my ribs with his elbow—so I put my fingers on the back of his neck. I don't know why I did that, but it just seemed like the right thing to do.

Then WHOOSH!—that Mustang almost stopped right beside us. Actually, it started slowing several yards up the road, but then skidded ten feet or so past me and Joel, spitting little chunks of gravel here and there. Then this massive cloud of trailing dust came roaring over us and the road, sort of blinding everything for a moment, and once it cleared, Dad was almost flying from that Mustang.

"It's him," Joel whispered.

"Yeah."

To be honest, aside from Dad, it was pretty strange to see the old car again. "The great American death car," Dad called it, on account of the fact that the previous owner and his wife had overdosed in the front seat. That's how Dad got it so incredibly cheap.

One-hundred and fifty-two dollars. Completely restored too. Dad loved telling the story. Seems the previous owner was a drug dealer from Childress. So him and his wife went out into the boonies to do some drugs. But the stuff they shot was bad and they both overdosed. The problem was, it was a week or so before anyone found them. It was summer. The windows were shut, and that pair of dead junkies just sat in there changing colors and getting funky. It still gives me the creeps thinking about it. I mean, Mom wouldn't even go near that car, but I was too little to know better. I couldn't say how many times I rode with Dad, just sitting right there where someone had got all dead and rotten. That's why no one on earth wanted to buy that car in the first place. I guess the guys at Pace Auto Sales could've sold it without telling anyone, but it stunk so bad. Dad said the Pace people had tried everything in the world to get rid of the stench. "Sickly sweet," was how Dad described it, though I don't remember it smelling so bad at all.

Anyway, Dad had on a wildass grin as he slammed the door on the Mustang, and even though it'd been a few years, he looked just about the same. He had on this white T-shirt and Wranglers and brown hiking boots. He wore the same damn blue Texas Rangers baseball cap I always imagine him having on, except it'd grown sort of stringy around the bill. I mean, it was like I'd just seen him yesterday or something. The only real difference was that his hair had got some gray and hung over his shoulders a bit.

I guess me and Joel didn't appear as happy as he thought we would be, because soon as he got about five feet away, that grin kind of evaporated. Then he just froze. And for a moment he just stood there, his head traveling up and down the length of me, then up and down the length of Joel, like he was trying to recall what we'd looked like before. It was almost as if he was deciding whether we was his sons or not. Then he went, "Hey, boys," like we was supposed to come running into his arms or something. But we didn't move an inch.

"What are you doing here?" I said, hoping maybe he'd get the idea I wasn't blown away by him just showing up.

Then Joel piped in with, "Hey, Dad," all quiet and friendly, which made Dad's mouth let out a nervous kind of laugh.

"Well, I wasn't about to go and see your mom," he told me. "I know better than that, don't I?" And I couldn't help it then, I had to smile some. I mean, just the idea of him ever coming close to Mom is sort of funny. Jesus, she'd tear into him without thinking twice.

Last time she saw him was at this Texaco station in Amarillo. This was a couple of years ago. It was well past midnight. Mom was coming home from work, but she'd gone to the station to get some aspirin first. Anyway, she came strolling from the ladies' room and noticed that Mustang by the pumps. Then she spotted Dad standing there giving his car the gas. He had his back to her. She said she knew it was him from the cap on his head. Before Dad figured what hit him, Mom had taken that hose straight from his hand. She just yanked the nozzle from the tank hole, gas running and all, and hosed Dad with as much gasoline as she could manage. Then she ran on inside that Texaco station to buy a lighter, but Dad didn't hang around for her to make the purchase. Can't say I blame him.

Dad turned and sort of shouted at the Mustang, "These here are my boys, babe!" And that's when I saw the woman with bleached-blond hair kind of watching from the passenger window. "That's Mary," Dad said.

Then Mary rolled the window down some, sort of stuck an arm in the air and fluttered her fingers, going, "Hey, boys," and I realized she was pretty young, like maybe twenty or twenty-two. But she was a real knockout, even from a distance I could tell that. So Joel and I gave her these quick greetings. Actually, we just lifted our hands real fast and then let them fall to our sides.

So then Dad stepped closer to us, and the way he was rubbing his palms together let me know he wasn't that comfortable. "Most of the rigs closed down in Borger," he said. "I figure

maybe I'm going to have to go out to California to find work."
Then he paused like we was supposed to say something, but we
didn't. We just stared at him with these blank expressions. So he
gave us this hopeless little wave of his right hand, saying, "I wanted
to see you before I left. Me and Mary been cruising around in
hopes I'd spot you coming or going."

Then he paused again. It about drove me nuts when he did
that. He kept bringing his fingers together, then pulling them
apart. Then he finally went, "I read about you in the paper,
Willy—guess you're really going places. Might go all the way to
the top, huh?"

"I don't know. Maybe."

Then Dad's voice got sort of defensive, which surprised both
me and Joel. He went, "Hey, I'm never going to be one of those
bastards that come out of the woodwork because his boy made
it big or something—I want you to know that. I don't want anything, now or ever. You know that?"

"I don't mind," I said, though I guess I was lying about that.

"Well, you're a hell of a kid," he told me. Then he told Joel,
"You are too—"

More silence. Joel started tracing a circle in the dirt with his
sneaker. As for me, to be totally honest, I couldn't take my eyes
from Dad. I kept looking for myself in that wrinkled, tanned face
of his. The thing was, he couldn't really return the stare. Maybe
he thought I was being mean or bitter. But I wasn't. I wasn't feeling nothing. And for a second his eyes met mine, and we was
locked on each other. Then he glanced at Joel, saying, "I guess I
should tell you I'm sorry. I mean, it just didn't work out for me to
hang on around here—and when I up and left, I always thought
maybe I could send for you or something—" His voice kind of
faded there. He took a deep gulp, and I was scared to death he was
going to start crying or carrying on. But he didn't. He just
sighed once, real heavy and long. Then he went, "Well—I guess
we better hit the road."

"Be careful," I said.

"Oh, I will." Then he offered me his right hand, Joel his left hand, and we all just sort of stood there shaking like crazy. Once that was done with, Dad said, "Wish I had some money for you or something, but it's been thin, you know—"

"We're okay," I told him.

He said, "Well, you two take it easy, okay?" And I could tell he was hesitant to leave. He didn't even move or anything. He just scratched the back of his neck. Then he nodded at both of us, took a couple of steps backwards, turned and headed toward that Mustang.

Truthfully, I was feeling kind of pitiful for him by then, so I said, "Hey, Dad?" And he stopped and glanced over at us. "You take care."

I mean, he just stayed there for what seemed forever. And it was almost like his face showed both relief and sadness, then he went on over to the Mustang, banged on the roof of that car twice, and said, "She's still running in fine form, boys."

And this is what strikes me as weird now: one second, a guy is taking a walk in the middle of nothing; the next second, he's watching his father's Ford Mustang driving away, his brother is crying beside him, and soon as that car dips over a hill, he's sobbing too.

I mean, Joel and I didn't say nothing to each other as we headed home. We just ambled along, wiping at our noses and stuff, and it was depressing as hell. To make matters worse, soon as we came into the house, Junie was sprawled all over the couch watching *Star Search*. So Joel went on into the bedroom, and I plopped down in the big recliner chair. By then my tears had dried, though it wouldn't have mattered one way or another to Junie. She was already sucked into the TV. She had her fingers in a box of Caramel Crunch. I could've been bleeding, squirting blood all over the place, and as long as I wasn't blocking her view she'd never notice.

Then Mom's voice came all puffy and panty from the hallway, saying, "Got to get going—see you people later." Then she was practically running into the living room wearing this tight, low-cut denim dress. Her hair was poofed like I'd never seen it before, all enormous and flammable. Her makeup was about three inches thick. It was like staring at Jamie Lynn twenty-five years down the road.

So I said, "Where you going?"

"Going out, hon. Got to serve a banquet."

And I guess the whole thing with Dad had me all screwed, because suddenly she bugged the shit out of me. She was always coming and going, carrying on like Joel and I didn't matter a bit. I mean, Mom is like a tornado that just blows through once or twice a day, shaking everything apart, and then leaves so everyone else can straighten the mess. So I told her, "Wouldn't kill you to stay home some night."

And she fixed me with that look of hers that says, "Watch your ass, kid," and she went, "Don't give me any crap, okay? I'm late!"

"Hey, why don't you hang around sometime?" I pointed at Junie, who wasn't watching *Star Search* no more. "Then you can put up with her shit instead of me and Joel!"

Junie's mouth fell open, and I swear there was chunks of Caramel Crunch on her tongue. "Fuck you, Willy," she said.

Mom started to wheel around on the heels of her pumps. "I don't have time for this now!"

That's when I went, "How come Dad left us?"

Mom dropped her purse. The insane thing was, it was like she was psychic or something. Her face got all twisted and freaky. "Son of a bitch! He's been here!"

"Yeah, he's been here! He wanted to see me and Joel!"

"I don't want him around here, you know that! Where is he?"

"He left!"

"When?"

"Today!"

"He damn well better not come around here!"

"How come he left us? Was it because you was never home then?"

Junie was sitting up on the couch by then. "You shit," she screamed, then threw that Caramel Crunch box right at me. I batted it away with my fist, scattering popcorn all over the carpet.

"Just shut up!" I told Junie, because it wasn't her damn argument to begin with.

"You shut up!"

But Mom was shaking her head. She didn't seem mad or nothing. Just lost. "So how come he left, Mom? Was it because you was always out getting saddled then too?"

Honestly, I didn't expect her eyes to well with tears. At that moment, I was wishing I'd done what Junie had said and shut up. But then Mom's voice got all menacing and kind of shaky with emotion. "If you think you know so much," she said, "why don't you go and live with the son of a bitch?"

I didn't know what to say. I figured I'd already said enough. "Aw, don't do this, you two," Junie was saying, but it was already too late.

Mom had me beat and she knew it. Then she was leaning over me in that chair, sounding angry, sort of taunting. Junie was standing behind her, trying to calm her by patting her arm, but Mom just elbowed Junie's hand away. "Well, did he?" she was saying to me. "Did he ask you to go with him?"

"No."

"Go live with the bastard! I don't give a shit!"

But I didn't say anything. And now I'm on the water tower. The thing is, there's this one incident that keeps coming to my mind. I don't know why. But before we lived in Claude, when we was living in Shamrock, I had a Labrador called Popeye, on account of the fact he had one eye. I was maybe six or seven then. Joel was just a baby. Our neighbors was these old folks known as the Braes. And Mrs. Braes had this chicken-wire hutch in their backyard, and she kept a huge black rabbit in it. Anyway, Dad and Mr. Braes wasn't getting along too well, because Popeye kept digging under their fence to get after that rabbit. So this one evening, Popeye comes home and he's got the Braes' rabbit in his mouth. And it's dead. Jesus, Mom and Dad about went nuts. Mom was saying Popeye needed to be put asleep. And Dad was saying there was no way he was going to put Popeye down, especially because of the Braes' stupid rabbit, which Mrs. Braes named Sweety.

But what happened was this: In the middle of the night, Mom snuck on into the Braes' backyard and just opened that hutch and put Sweety back inside. Her and Dad figured that because Popeye hadn't made a mess of the rabbit, the Braes would think Sweety just died a natural kind of death. And I guess it would've worked fine, except Sweety had already died a natural kind of death that morning. Mrs. Braes had found the rabbit in the cage, and Mr. Braes had buried Sweety somewhere. Then Popeye dug the rabbit up, brought it home to us, and that's what Mom and Dad didn't know.

Anyway, when Mrs. Braes saw her just-buried Sweety in that hutch the next morning, she almost had a heart attack. And pretty soon Mr. Braes figured everything out and came banging on the front door. I mean, Dad kept explaining to that old man how it wasn't really him or Mom's fault. He told Mr. Braes that no harm was meant. But Mom felt real awful, and she blamed Popeye.

And what I can't get out of my head is the memory of Mom and me standing at the kitchen window in our Shamrock house. She had her hands on my shoulders. We was watching Dad with Popeye in the backyard. And Popeye was jumping all over him, just acting like dogs do. And Dad was petting Popeye on the head, scratching behind his ears, and then he told Popeye to sit. And Popeye was a good dog, because he sat right away. I swear I didn't see the gun ever. All I heard was this CRACK! There wasn't no blood or nothing. It was like Popeye just buckled forward on his front legs and went to sleep. And what I remember Mom saying was, "Good," which didn't seem right at all because he was my dog.

The worst part was Dad. He spent the better part of the evening out there with that dead dog. He had some beer. Mom wouldn't let me go into the backyard, but I could look through the window. And I did. I folded my arms across the sill, watching as Dad drank beer after beer. I saw him take the bullets left in that gun and toss them around the yard. Then he took that gun apart, piece by piece, and got rid of the parts in the same manner as the bullets. Then finally he just stretched out alongside Popeye in the tall grass. And that's how he stayed for the rest of the night. The next morning, when I went to the window, Popeye and Dad was gone. Dad came home a couple of weeks later. Popeye never did.

Dead Flowers

This afternoon, Coach Bud finished his before-practice lecture with, "We got one more, boys—just one more before the play-offs. I want you to listen up real good right now! The one thing we can't do is to be packing our bags before we get our ticket. Everybody is talking about how Jayton's got by on the skin of their teeth while we been swamping all the others, but the bottom line is this—they hadn't been beat in the district just like we hadn't been beat in the district—and that makes us dead even going into Friday night. The winner goes on and plays with the whole state watching—and the losers tuck tail and stay home! It's as simple as that! We can't win a playoff game until we get to the playoffs, and soon as you go taking something for granted, that's when we get our butts knocked right out of the party—and when the game's over, it's over! It's too damn late to look back and say 'we could've' or 'we should've'—when it's over, it's over! There ain't no prizes for second best."

And I guess what Coach Bud had said sunk in on us all pretty good, because we practiced without fault. We didn't goober a single play, and Coach Bud was grinning all over the field. He kept clapping his hands. He kept shouting, "That's it, boys! You got it!"

And even though the clouds had turned sort of massive and dark above, and there was this sharp breeze scooting through my gear, we didn't let that faze us a bit. I think we all felt like we had Jayton's number, and my knee operated like it was bionic or something. And after practice, when some of us was showering, Lee started singing that "Like a Rock" song. I mean, Lee don't have that nice of a voice or nothing, but the way he was carrying on seemed sort of accurate for the moment. Forget that we was all naked and soapy and going, "Like a rock—like a rock—like a rock—" which was the only part of that tune any of us knew anyhow.

Life seemed sort of okay when I pushed through that gym door and stepped outside. The sky was spitting a mixture of rain and snow, but it didn't seem so cold at all. Soon as that snow hit the asphalt, them white flecks did what I imagine those *Star Trek* transporter people do when they go from the *Enterprise* to some planet—the flakes kind of sat there for a moment, then vaporized. "Molecular breakdown," is how Joel once explained all that transporter stuff.

Anyway, I knew Hanna was going to be pissed when I came walking across the school parking lot, so I just took it leisurely getting over to the truck. I kind of gazed up into that wannabe blizzard for a second, watching as them flakes sailed toward me. Then I stuck my tongue out and tried to catch some snow on the tip. But while I was enjoying the weather, Hanna tilted the rearview in my truck so I could be aware of her glarey eyes squinting, suggesting something like, "It ain't fair I've got to wait on you."

And soon as I opened the door and climbed in, she started with, "Where've you been? I finished studying in the library ages ago. I been sitting here waiting for nearly an hour," which wasn't totally true. More like twenty minutes she'd been waiting. Her face was all pouty. She dumped my truck keys in my lap. But I acted dumb like I do.

"I was talking to Coach," I told her, closing the door. Then I slumped back against the seat.

"Well, I got to go straight home now. I'm already late for supper."

The truth was, I wasn't in the mood to be with her anyway. She just stirs the shit in me these days, going on and on about how I should do this or go to college here and blah blah blah. I mean, I had a lot on my mind, what with all Coach Bud had said about Friday's game. But I didn't want her to get all ruffled and all, even though she already was. So I just put on the Willy Show. I gave her a sweet smile that said, "I'm sorry." I rested a hand on one of her hands. I went, "Can we go riding around a little while?"

"No, we can't! I told you I was late for supper!" And she was looking real fine. Her hair was pulled into a ponytail. She'd got her lips colored with this waxy gunk she called Vermilion Dusk. She had on a gray sweatshirt of mine, the one with the Fighting Irishman on the front, and that shirt was bunched all baggy at her waist. To be honest, she made it kind of hard to fake the Willy Show.

I said, "I just want to talk to you a little while," except the only thing I really wanted to do was grab a Coke at the Exxon and hit the road home. I leaned against her and got a good whiff of that sweatshirt, which reeked of this bad combination of Hanna's Night Musk perfume and my ancient body odor. I mean, when I gave her that shirt last summer, I figured she'd have washed it or something.

She whined, "I guess you could've been talking to me instead of Coach."

"Come on. Cut it out. Coach Bud said there's going to be more scouts here Friday for the game." Man, I was lying through the gaps in my teeth. If I'd been completely up-front, I'd have gone, "I knew you was out here in the truck. And I bet you're kind of cold. But I just wasn't too excited about seeing you. I'm just a jerk, and what's worse, I don't feel that bad about it either. I could've been here thirty minutes ago, but I just hung around Coach's office talking about almost nothing. I knew you'd be all hyper and wound tight, and I guess that's how I wanted you to get."

Then she just kicked in with, "You know you can go to Tech with me. I don't know why you keep talking about it," and that's when the Willy Show went limp.

"Coach said I—"

"Coach Bud! Coach Bud! What is he, your daddy?" And she said that in a mimicky way, her voice all high and sort of screechy, could've busted an eardrum. I swear I almost considered booting her butt right through that passenger door then. But I didn't.

The drive to her house was as rotten as can be. Hanna kept her arms folded under her boobs. She stared straight ahead at the snow blowing across the windshield. I turned the radio on, but I couldn't find any good songs playing. So what I did was set the dial on static, just crackle and hiss, and edged the volume up some. I kept waiting for Hanna to reach over and switch the damn thing off, but she didn't. And after two minutes of that noise, I kind of wished she had.

Anyway, once I got to her house, Hanna about jumped from the truck. And before I could say a word, she'd dug this folded piece of notebook paper from a pocket and tossed it on my dashboard. "I wrote you a poem," she said. Then she slammed the door and trudged on across the lawn toward the front porch. She didn't look back or nothing, so I pulled away from the curb all slow, half expecting her to wave or something. I twisted the volume down on the radio, and suddenly I was getting warm and comfortable inside, sort of how it feels when school lets out for summer. But when I glanced into the rearview, I spotted Mrs. Lockhart standing on the porch, wiping her hands clean on her yellow apron, and Hanna was heading up the steps pretty fast. And I could tell something was being said, because soon as Hanna got close to Mrs. Lockhart, they was all hugs. The snow was coming a little harder then, but I still got a good view of Mrs. Lockhart just holding Hanna there. She was holding her daughter real close.

The thing is, who am I kidding? I know there ain't no future for me and her. Her daddy knows it. Coach Bud knows it. And even if ol' Waylon didn't have it in for me, I'd probably still be tired of her by now. What's worse, Hanna just doesn't understand when to shut up. I mean, today's speech from Coach Bud was important, but she never asked me about that. She never wants to hear what I hear. It's always, "Willy, I done this," or, "Willy, you should do this," or, the line that makes me want to spit, "What I think is wrong with you, Willy, is this." It's enough to push a guy into insanity.

So then the Duke was riding alongside yours truly, flipping that triangled wedge of notebook paper between his fingers like a quarter, going, "Son, there's a time to move on, and I think this is it." Then he fired that wedge into the air with his thumb and it ricocheted against the roof of the truck and came soaring into my shirt pocket.

"You're right," I told him. "Dammit if you ain't right."

Even Coach Bud was saying after practice, "Willy, I understand you got feelings for Waylon's daughter, but don't get your head all bunged up with this idea of love." I was sitting in his office like I do sometimes after practice. He was pointing at a paperback on his desk called *The Power of Positive Thinking*. "Got to stay focused. Your future is at hand. I don't want you to take no offense by this, but there's going to be lots of women along the road for you. Tons of them. Let's not get bogged down in this idea of being in love. To tell the truth, there ain't a high school student in the world that's ever been in love. It's just hormones flying around. It's the idea of love that they're in love with. The idea of love." I ain't too sure what he meant by that, but I had to agree with him anyway.

So now I'm at a table inside Whitey Fontane's Exxon station. It ain't like this is a café or anything close, but old Whitey keeps a card table in the back so the Domino Men have somewhere to play when the parlor doors swing shut for the night. I figure those craggy cowboys keep Whitey's store running almost as much as those folks traveling on 287 who stop in Claude for gas. I think that's why Whitey has two or three boxes of jawbreakers stacked beside the cash register. He also has a cooler on the floor by the counter just filled with bottles of Orange Crush. It don't matter if it's a million below zero outside, Whitey still has that cooler filled with ice. Don't ask me why, but Domino Men love jawbreakers and Orange Crush.

What gets me going about Whitey is that he's black. I've never asked him, but ten bucks says that ain't his real name. Maybe he just got called Whitey because he's the only black man in town who owns a business. That's how it is here. If a guy's fat, someone just might label him Slim. Joel's pal Chubby is about as skinny as skinny can be, and his honest name is Charlie. The thing is, a kid gets stuck with something like Chubby or Slim or Whitey early on, no matter if he likes the sound of it or not, and he'll be called that the rest of his life. Don't matter if he becomes President of the United States or something, Chubby will always be Chubby in Claude.

Anyway, so I'm at this table killing an hour or so until the snow takes a break. I've gone through two cans of Coke, and now I'm on my third. I got that poem Hanna wrote spread before me, but I'm stacking dominos on top of it. And I'm building me a tiny dream home, though it don't look like much. Whitey's in the garage working on some wreck of a Camaro he found in a Childress junkyard, but he left a portable electric heater humming on the floor nearby. I swear my Wranglers feel like they're getting sunburned.

"Hi, Willy," this voice says, and I glance up at Jackie Maitland, who's coming on into the station. "I thought that was your truck out there." He's rubbing his hands together, sort of shaking the snow from his Polo sweater.

"Hey, Jackie," I say, then I notice he's got his camera hung around his neck. "Taking pictures?"

"The weather's good for black and white," he says. "Do you mind?" Then he's aiming that camera in my direction. He's focusing the lens.

"What should I do?"

"Nothing. Just be Willy."

So I hover my chin above my domino castle. I get a stupid

face going like I'm some geek or a retarded guy. I cock an eye-brow. And soon as that shutter snaps, I blink. "I blew it!"

"It was great," Jackie says, stepping near the heater to warm himself. "Perfect."

So I go, "The roads bad enough to keep you in town?"

But only one side of his face smiles. "No. But that's what I'll tell Dad."

"You want to sit down?"

"Yeah, okay."

He crosses to the table and slides into the chair across from me. As he takes the camera from his neck and sets it on the table, I brush away my domino home. Then I push Hanna's poem at him. "This make any sense to you?" I watch his black eyes get narrow and almost crossed as he takes the notebook paper. His face gets real studious, kind of intense, like he's examining every goddamn word on the page.

> FLOWERS, DEAD AND GONE
> Once was the day of Love,
> but no more, or so it seems.
> Am I no longer your heart's
> one true desire? Oh, I wonder.
> The flowers beside my bed once
> were full, bright, of many colors,
> though now are dry and withered,
> like the weathered hands of Death.
> Was it always like this?
> Come home, my love. I am waiting.
> Bring me fresh cut flowers for the vase.
> Let us be lovers untouched by time;
> a leaf falls near winter,
> but why should we?

Finally, Jackie puts the paper down and goes, "It's a poem."

"I know it's a poem," I tell him, "but what does it mean?"

So he studies it a bit more. "Hanna wrote this?"

"Yeah."

"Well, I'd say it's kind of a love poem, except the girl misses the guy. The guy's gone off somewhere."

"That's what you get?"

He shrugs. "I guess." Then he shoves that poem on over to me. Then we just sit here with only that heater making any noise. And it's weird, because suddenly it's like we're both nervous or something. Jackie brings his fingers to that camera. He fiddles with the strap. I sip on my Coke and stare outside. It's already getting dark, though the snow has eased some. Then Jackie says, "Big game Friday, huh?"

So I go, "I guess they all are," but it comes out sounding sort of snotty, not at all like I meant it to. I mean, it is a big game. It's like my whole life is riding on Friday night. Part of me is excited as a kid with a mouthful of Gummi Worms, but the other part wants to shit itself and hide. But a guy like Jackie, he's set. He don't have to worry about playing Jayton or what college wants him and all that stuff. "At least you don't have to wonder, do you, Jackie?"

And his face gets sort of odd and confused, like I've said something horrible. Like I've just told him his mother got crushed under a tanker or something worse. "What do you mean?"

"Your ranch. I mean, when you get out of school, you don't have to do anything else."

Then he gets a bitter expression. "I'll never have anything to do with that place," he says. "I hate that place."

That about blows me away. "It's the biggest ranch in the county," I say.

And he goes, "Yeah, it is, I guess," and I half expect him to add, "So what?"

"I'd sure take it," I tell him. "I'd go out on that ranch and never leave."

And it's like someone just deflated the air from his body. He kind of sags in that chair. And for a second he has these puppy eyes, sort of round and sad at once. "Dad wouldn't have me around there anyhow—even if I wanted to."

"Hey, I know you and your dad don't get on too well, but hell—it's like all of us—everybody else, you know?"

And for a while we stay quiet. Jackie just keeps his head downward, and I kind of tinker with the dominos. Then he goes, "You know what, Willy? My dad thinks I'm a—" But he doesn't finish.

"A what?"

And it's like he wants so bad to tell me something, and I think I know what it is. But I ain't so sure I want to hear it. Jackie gazes through that window next to the table, then he just sighs. "Nothing. I just hear him and my mom yelling at each other about me all the time."

"I know about that," I say, trying to just skirt the issue, and that makes him grin some. So then I go, "Aw, hell, Jackie, you're okay—just like you are—you're okay—"

And it's like we don't got much else to say then. I look at my feet in them grubby boots. They're burning from that heater. It's like I don't got feet no more because all I feel is heat instead of toes. And I want to crumple Hanna's stupid poem about dead flowers because it don't make any sense, and I don't like poetry anyway.

Then Jackie suddenly grabs that camera from the table. He sticks it to his face, he's focusing like crazy, and SNAP! "Smile, Willy," he says. And I do. SNAP!

Chipping at E

I come from my bedroom to find Mom and Stump on the couch. Earlier I'd come from my bedroom and found Bob and Junie on the couch. Mom and Stump was gone then, but Joel was on the floor with his eyes glued to the tube. Now it's Mom and Stump, and Joel's still there like he hasn't moved at all. Junie's curled in the big chair, and she's asleep. Bob's gone. Mom's watching *Viva Las Vegas* on the late show. She's got on her pink robe and Snoopy Dog slippers. She's got popcorn in a bowl on her lap. Stump's poring over the sports section of the newspaper. He can't stand Elvis, but Mom makes him sit through those movies when they're on. But Stump will only do it if he can read the newspaper and nurse a Coors six-pack. From the look of things, what with the cans crushed around Stump's boots, the rest of the newspaper heaped between him and Mom, I'd say that movie was almost done.

Mom and Stump have had some pretty nasty arguments because of Elvis. "You got to love E," Mom sometimes says. She doesn't call him Elvis anymore. Don't ask me why.

"Don't got to love nobody," is what Stump will tell her. And that's usually how the fights begin.

When Stump realizes I'm standing near the couch, he brings that sports section down and goes, "Hey, here's the hoss."

Mom hasn't spoken to me since the other day when we'd flown off the handle at each other, so she just gives me this sulky glance before turning her attention around to the King. So I kind of stroll on over to Joel and scuff his head, but Joel just waves once without taking his face from the TV.

Next thing I know, Stump is on his feet. "Need to talk to you."
He's got me by an elbow. He's pulling me with him into a corner
of the living room. Then he leans close, sort of lowers his voice
some, and the beer stink shooting from his mouth wants to
knock me out. He's saying, "Me and Bob going to make a run over
to Jayton on Thursday—see who we can stir up." Then he gives
me this wink. "Now, listen, Willy, you tell me straight. You figure
you boys can take them by twenty-one? I'm telling you if we give
them twenty-one points we can hit the feed lot and the Four Sixes
ranch and get a grand going easy on this one. You figure twenty-
one is safe? Hell, you can make that spread yourself—you figure?"

"Yeah, probably—"

He clamps a hand on my left shoulder, gives me a quick
squeeze with his fingers. "Hotdammit, we're going to do it," he
says. "Hell, I'll hock my guns on this one." Then he gives my left
shoulder another squeeze. And his fingers on my right elbow grip
a little harder. And it strikes me as being strange that we're
standing like this. I mean, if someone was to peek through the
window from outside, they'd think Stump was giving me a dancing lesson or something. "We'll remember you on it," he tells me.
"Don't we always?"

"Sure, Stump," I say.

"You're a real hoss." Then that beer stench carries Stump on
past me. He wheels on behind the couch, bends down, and
kisses Mom on her head. "Got to run, babe! I'll talk to you later!"

And someone would've expected Mom to get annoyed then,
but she didn't. She was too caught up in what Elvis was doing to
be bothered. One second, Stump's pressing his nasty lips to her
hair. Next second, the screen door is clapping shut. But Stump's
breath just kind of still hangs around.

Now Elvis is punching some guy. A few minutes ago he was
singing. I find myself on the couch with Mom, who's trying her
damnedest to pretend I don't exist no more. I reach for the popcorn, but she pushes my hand away. Then she gets all huffy and
sticks that bowl between us. And for a moment I get a crazy idea

to jump in front of the TV. I'd just hop up there and start shaking my legs like Elvis. I bet that'd drive her insane. Willy as E, going, "I just want to send this one out to my mama," then I'd launch into "Don't Be Cruel" or "That's All Right, Mama" or something wild like that. But then I recall how once when Mom was drunk she told me and Stump that her and her girl cousins used to get wet watching Elvis. She said that when the King was on Ed Sullivan, just gyrating and carrying on, her and her cousins could've thrown their panties against the wall and made them stick. And when I think about Mom saying that, the last thing I want to do is stand in front of her being Elvis.

Anyway, when the credits finally roll, I say, "Hey, Mom, I'm sorry about—" but she just takes the remote and begins flipping here and there. "Can I talk to you a few minutes?" Then I notice Joel is staring right at us. And Junie's kind of stirring in the big chair. "I mean out of here somewhere?"

But Mom goes, "Seems like you been doing enough talking to me of late," and she says that without even giving me another glance.

Truthfully, it doesn't bug me much. I know how she is. She'll go on being mad for a couple more days. She'll throw some of my things around, like my comb in the bathroom. I'll find it in the tub, or on the floor by the toilet. She'll cook her and Joel and Stump dinner, something she can't afford like steak, but won't make any for me. Then out of the blue she'll be, "Hey, hon, how's practice? How you doing? You going to make me proud Friday?" And it'll be like nothing ever happened. See, as long as Pug's been my mother, I ain't ever heard her say sorry once. But I'm used to it. When I was a kid, it about tore at me when she acted mean like that. Now I could hardly give a crap.

I climb from the couch without saying anything else and go to my bedroom. Joel follows. I stretch out on my bunk, and he gets on the ladder leading to his bed. But he just stands there, resting his head on a rung, arms folded under his chin. "She'll get over it," he says.

"I know. I ain't worried."

"You look worried."

"Well, I ain't." And I'm tempted to tell Joel about what I do when Mom gets mean. But I probably won't. He doesn't know I'm waiting for Junie to go home. Soon as Junie leaves, Mom hits the sack. Then I do my business. I take that Elvis Commemorative Gold-Plated Dish from the living room wall. I find a butter knife in the kitchen. Then I chip away some of that gold-plating from the outer portion. Not too much. Just enough to make me feel better. I scrape it over the sink and wash the damage into the disposal. She hasn't ever noticed either, though I do it a lot these days.

"You going to bed?" Joel says.

"Not yet."

And what's funny is, I can tell Joel is growing. Used to be when he was on that ladder looking down at me, the length of his body covered about four of them rungs. Now he's almost five rungs tall.

"Tell me something, Joel."

"What?"

"I don't know. Just something."

His face gets scrunched. I can tell he's thinking pretty hard. Then he goes, "Oh, did you know that there's no way to know why someone who snores can't hear it? It's true."

And that cracks me up some. And it cracks Joel up too. And we're like two idiots just giggling in our room. And after a while, I reach at the ladder for one of his big toes. I kind of twist it, but in a gentle way. I just hold on to that toe and wait for the sounds of the screen door banging after Junie, and then for Mom's Snoopy Dog slippers to come padding along the hallway.

Lighting Pall Malls

It's this fingernail-moon of a night, so those cows ain't too easy to spot at first. Bunch of dim blobs here and there. Wide patches shifting among them barren mesquite trees. For some reason they remind me of zombies, sort of ambling along and eating, which is pretty creepy to think about. Me and Hanna are parked in my Chevy by that hidden feed trail pasture, and I've been watching them cows come forward for about ten minutes or so. Somewhere there's a gate left open, or a downed fence row. It's like these Here-fords got no idea what's in store for them, so they're making their escape real slow. If I was one of those cows, I'd be running like hell. I'd be kicking at the moon and mooing and going psycho. I'd get as far as I could from Claude and all them slaughterhouses in Amarillo. I'd find me some lonesome Caprock cowboy and bite him hard enough to draw blood. Then I'd stomp him to death. That'd be the kind of cow I'd be.

Anyway, Hanna is slumped against the door on the passenger side. She's got a chunk of tissue wadded in a hand, which is prob-ably damp from her snot and tears. She keeps having me turn on the cab light so she can check her Swatch, though I don't know why. And she's been crying, just sniffle sniffle, while them cows graze toward the truck.

She's saying, "You could've told me what Daddy said, you could've just told me—"

And I don't know what that's about, because I just got done telling her everything. I explained how her dad got me in that Yugo, and how he'd said I probably shouldn't tell no one about our conversation. I even mentioned that ol' Waylon had sung along to a Rosanne Cash song on the radio, and she said, "He doesn't even know who she is."

She goes, "You haven't even talked to me all week—"

"I've talked to you."

So she sighs all raggedy through her nose, because her head is clogged. "We're going to keep going out together this year, aren't we? Even if we don't go to college together?" Then her voice gets sort of weepy. She's saying, "All I've ever been with is you! We do have the rest of the year!"

And this is where I'm supposed to tell her what I was hoping she'd tell me. It's like, Jesus, just ignore some girl, don't treat her like nothing special in front of her friends, sit across the table from her at lunch, explain there's no time to talk to her after school because of football practice, avoid her phone calls, stick her poetry in the kitchen trash, explain to her that her dad is a bastard, tell her the old guy goes out of his way to bug a fellow on a nice afternoon, wake her in the middle of the night, make damn sure she knows that Texas Tech ain't the school for a college football player, then wait for her to say, "It's over. I can't stand you." But it ain't happening like that. She's just staring at me all flustered and bitter and a little fearful.

And suddenly I don't want to be here no more. I want to climb that water tower and dangle my legs from the catwalk. I picture myself sitting right under that peeling green E in that big CLAUDE mural, just feeling the cold and bundling in my jacket and shivering some. That water tower hums with power when I'm there, but I don't know why. And there's all this graffiti sprayed and scratched all over the place, lots of scraped hearts and the names of a few people I've never heard of, and some of the dates around those names are as old as forty years or more. Up there, if I squint my eyes a bit, the streetlights look like stars. And in the middle of the night, there's a big nothing of blackness around the edge of town that seems to stretch into forever.

"Willy—" Hanna says. She's dabbing her cheeks with that bunch of tissue. Then she doesn't say another word.

I got my stare aimed through the windshield. I'm focusing on the one Hereford who's made it to the grill of my truck. And now I can't think of nothing except that big wind that brought me into Amarillo yesterday night. And I know this is what Hanna should know, but I don't got the guts to just open my mouth and say what happened.

I'd had a dream about Ramona. First I was in that Royal Hotel corridor outside her door. And this guy came walking all fast from her room, except I didn't catch his face or even get how old he was. But I noticed that he kept fiddling with the necktie he wore that had all these butterfly pictures on it. And the butterflies were all different. Some were wide and others were small. The silly thing was, he'd yank that tie to the side, making it all whompyjawed. But that tie would just fix itself, sort of straighten out, and soon as it did that, the guy would mess it up again. Then I was in her room, except I was kind of in the air, I guess. I watched her through the spinning blades of this ceiling fan, though she doesn't actually have one of those. Anyway, Ramona had on a leather skirt and a baggy T-shirt and she kept closing her door and then opening it and then closing it and then opening it. And I don't know how long that went on, but then she just kind of appeared right below me. She stood in the middle of that room, except it wasn't really her room because the floor had got covered in shiny linoleum. And she sort of sunk to her knees. Then she stretched on her back. And it was like she didn't have no idea I was around. She took a deep, deep breath. And then this little kitten came over to her. It meowed and rubbed against an arm and purred like a happy cat does. But she just pushed it away. Then that kitten returned, but it wasn't a kitten no more. It was this huge old fat cat. But it still purred and rubbed and stuff. And Ramona just kicked at it with her foot. And then it became a rooster, except she didn't have to knock it away or nothing, because as soon as that cat switched to a rooster, it shot across that slick floor and was gone. Then Ramona brought her hand to her mouth. She gulped in her throat, and I thought she was about to vomit or something. But she didn't. And I'm glad she didn't. Then she moved her hand to those thick lips. And there was also this wind beating against the walls and rattling glass somewhere. Those walls breathed with her. When she'd suck in, the walls sucked in. But none of that seemed to matter to her. She just tucked her hair behind her neck. Then her eyes closed. Her hands slipped under that shirt. And it was like I was riding behind those fingertips, spying as she touched her boobs and tummy. Then that wind howled like nuts, just shaking everything, and I stirred in my bed.

There was a screaming southwester beating all over the house. The windows in my bedroom whistled some with that lonesome wind. And my dick was hard and bent funny in my shorts. The clock on the dresser showed 12:23 A.M. Next thing I knew, that southwester had chased me along 287 and sailed my butt on into the Royal Hotel. Of course, I'd showered by then, got my hair just perfect, put on some pressed Wranglers. But my insides just tingled around like a ton of electric wires had snapped or something, so I stepped on into that bar by the lobby called Roughnecks.

To be honest, it wasn't much of a bar: a pool table, maybe a few chairs, an unplugged jukebox with shitty songs on it anyway. Not a lot to study there. It was dark as pitch. The brown wall behind the bar had a couple of black-and-white posters showing Arnold Schwarzenegger flexing on a beach somewhere, but they were both the same. And the place stunk too. It smelled like this mixture of body odor and rotten eggs. I ain't joking.

But the bartender treated me nice. He was just a friendly, sort of agreeable older fellow, with his head shaved bald, and an insane curlycue mustache like some guy from the turn of the century or before. He didn't ask my age or nothing when I ordered a Red Dog. He didn't even seem to mind me being his only customer. He just dried these beer mugs with a rag, sometimes bringing that rag to his forehead for a swipe, and when I asked him why his T-shirt read *Caution: Uncontrollable Flame,* he just smiled and went, "Funny," like I was his best friend or someone.

Then after my second or third beer, while I was gazing at my reflection on the glass of this empty bottle, just as my whole body started getting flushed and peaceful, Curlycue set another Red Dog in front of me. "Here," he said, "it's on me."

"Thanks," I told him, kind of surprised and grateful at once, and he gave me a wink that said, "No problem."

Then this huge gust bellowed along the street outside, scouring dirt across the front window of Roughnecks, sort of rumbling the place with its passing. And Curlycue sighed hard through his nostrils, then said, "Something's blowing in. Something big."

"Yeah—" and I hoisted that new bottle and drank until the foam filled my throat.

And Curlycue put his elbows on the counter, kind of watching me chug some, and when I brought that bottle down, he went, "Been here before?"

But I didn't know if he meant the Royal or Roughnecks, so I just said, "Yeah."

"Slow night. That wind ain't helping much either."

That's about when these two fellows came waltzing on into the place. And soon as Curlycue spotted them, he grabbed this broom by the cash register and started sweeping like nuts. And one of those fellows was all Mr. Polyester Slacks; he had a goofy yellow shirt, sort of silky, with all these river boats and orange sunsets painted on it. And the other guy was just a lardass biker, all black leather and chains, with this Moses beard and everything. I mean, Jesus, it was way past midnight but Biker Guy had sunglasses on. So then Mr. Polyester Slacks looked me over real good as he stood at the bar, but I just sipped my beer without giving him much attention.

"Getting nasty out there," Curlycue said to those goobers while he swept and swept.

But Mr. Polyester Slacks could've cared less about the weather.

He was too busy jerking a thumb in my direction, going, "How old is he?"

Then Curlycue got all nervous as hell. He quit brooming, and his fingers tightened on the handle. Then his voice kind of stammered as he went, "Ah, he's legal, Deke. I checked him out."

So I just hunkered my head some, sort of avoiding any eye contact. And I half expected to get busted, but Mr. Polyester Slacks didn't pay me no more mind. He asked Curlycue, "Receipts?"

"On your desk."

And that was that. When I glanced up, that pair was crossing through the bar, moving toward this door in the back. Then they was gone. And Curlycue seemed a bit relieved once they'd disappeared. He kind of shrugged his shoulders. He set that broom aside, saying in a whispery tone, "Our little secret."

"You bet," I told him.

The truth was, I didn't feel so hot then. My stomach just wouldn't lay off with the swishing and bubbling and blurping. I think it might have been all those beers. Or maybe it had something to do with the idea of seeing Ramona again. Anyway, Curlycue kept trying to make conversation with me, but I didn't pay much attention. He went, "You from here?"

"Claude."

"Sorry to hear that. Got the shit kicked out of me in Claude once."

"Sorry—"

"Me too."

Then bile began lifting to my throat, sort of burning and tasting evil, so I forced it down with more beer. I had that vomity sensation, all twisty inside and gross. So I took in these long breaths, but that didn't help much. So I shut my eyes. That's when everything got worse. My stomach started pressing in on itself, sort of pushing all the crap I'd swallowed toward my mouth. Then I heard Curlycue go, "You all right, son?"

"I ain't so sure," I said, cracking an eye.

Then Curlycue motioned some with a hand, kind of sweeping at me with his fingers. "If you're about to be sick, don't do it here. The powder room is left of the jukebox, okay?"

Now, let me mention this right here—I've stood in some skanky bathrooms before, but the john in Roughnecks about takes the prize. Just a single dusty lightbulb lit the damn place, so it was dim as hell. And my boots kind of squished over those tiles. And I had to hold my breath some from that humid pee stench. I mean, someone might've thought a bunch a guys just got it into their goofy minds to skip the urinals and piss on the floor and in the sinks instead. Shit, I won't even mention the toilets, except to say they was mostly spattered brown and clogged with chunks of TP.

Anyway, I dropped to my knees in this one stall. I bent over that nasty bowl, and I waited and waited for my innards to explode past my lips. But nothing like that happened. So I stuck a finger in my throat, sort of shook it around the tonsils, just hoping I'd gag that vomit or whatever out, but all I did was cough up some bile. And I guess that helped, because suddenly my guts settled. Then I burped like crazy. Just burp burp burp.

So soon as I got to feeling better, I spotted all these things written and drawn on the walls of that stall. Someone had taken a black marker and made a picture of a big ol' butt. And under that butt were the words: COME ON, OPEN MY ASS! But that wasn't all. I won't bother to describe the other drawings, but there was about a ton of sayings, most of which made no sense—

EXOTIC BARELY LEGAL SLUTS & SEX RECORDING
COLLEGE BOY LIKES GUYZ
FAT WOMEN RULE
ASS & PANTY WORSHIP CLUB
BARBARA LOVES LIZA
FART SNIFFING, FACE SITTING
SKINNY MEANS MORE SEX!!!!!!!!!!

There was so much of that stupid stuff that I had to laugh. It was downright hilarious. Just the thought of someone taking the time to put all that crap on those walls got me going pretty good. I mean, forget that three minutes before I was about to barf.

And sitting right there on that funky floor, I got to remembering Mr. Callahorn, who taught Civics for a year at Claude when I was a freshman. I don't recall exactly how it came about, but one day he hauled off and told the class that the government had all kinds of sneaky schemes going on that our parents didn't realize they was paying for. He said top-secret UFO projects were being conducted in the New Mexican desert, and that the military was killing ranch cattle in the middle of the night. He said Martin Luther King Jr. was a communist working for JFK, and that Muhammad Ali had shot Malcolm X as a favor for President Johnson. He explained that all the dirty, filthy words and pictures put on bathroom walls came from government employees. He told us that the government paid people to do that. And when Lee said, "Sounds like a good job," I thought Mr. Callahorn was going to brain him.

Anyway, my head was spinning some when I left that stall, but my stomach had relaxed a bit. I went to a sink and turned the faucet on. And from the cool trickle, I rinsed my face all over. I scooped water into my mouth and gargled and spit. I found a stick of gum in my pocket and chewed so fast that my jaw got sore real quick. And even though I still felt a little uneasy inside, I must've looked a whole lot better when I stepped from that bathroom, because Curlycue went, "The frog has returned a prince!"

And before I left Roughnecks to go on upstairs to see Ramona, Curlycue gave me a napkin with his phone number written on it, which was a decent kind of thing to do considering how woozy I was. He said, "Just in case you can't make it home, or you need some coffee or something. I'm closing here in about ten minutes. But call anytime you want."

"Thanks," I told him. "I appreciate it."

Then I ambled on into the hotel lobby. And for a moment I just stood by the glass window there, watching as trash and newspaper got tumbled along the street by the wind. And in the reflection I saw that huge black clerk behind the check-in desk. So when I turned around, as I was walking across the lobby toward the stairs, I noticed he had his nose buried in the exact same copy of *Penthouse* I'd seen him flipping through the night I'd brought Ramona from Claude. He had a portable radio on that desk too, playing this scratchy and jazzy-sounding music, and the tan Indiana Jones hat he wore was sort of scrunched over his brow so a fellow couldn't really see his face. To be honest, he appeared sort of shady, just wide and dark and mean, with thick knuckles and gold rings and a ratty old undershirt. And as I headed up those stairs, I heard him giggling to himself. He just carried on and on, like those bloodshot eyes of his had suddenly found the world's funniest thing on some page of that magazine.

The door to 219 had been left unlocked, and that chilly breeze whipped through Ramona's room on into the corridor. At first she wasn't nowhere to be seen, so I just said her name a couple of times, not too loud because I didn't want to scare her or nothing. She had some laundry hanging over a chair by this lifted window, allowing the air to scoot around a couple of pullovers, a pair of pearl-colored panties, four black socks. And when I said her name again, Ramona came slowly from the bathroom in that white robe of hers.

"Who is it?" she said, sounding a little worried. But when she saw it was only me, this almost relieved expression sort of spread across her face, all tired and worn.

And it was weird because then she almost yanked me into the room without saying another word. Then she closed that door. And next thing I knew, we're standing on that scatter rug by the kitchenette. Jesus Christ, my hands were joggling like crazy. And I just stared as she shrugged that robe from her shoulders, letting it slip all the way past her body to the floor. Then she was naked as could be, and I think maybe my mouth hung down like a goon. But she was gazing right into my eyes, and that downcast expression had all but disappeared. Then she hugged into me, putting her head on my shoulder. So I put my arms around her back, pressing on that nice skin, which had gotten all rough and goosefleshy from that breeze shooting in at us. And with my hands trembling something awful, I was hoping she'd figure I was just cold and nothing else.

To be truthful, I didn't know what to do, so I started urging us toward the mattress. But Ramona kept resisting, except not rudely or nothing. "No," she whispered, and I wasn't too sure what she meant by that. Then she kind of pushed me away. Then she had her fingers on my shirt buttons. Then those fingers went to my Wranglers. And I had a boner the size of Texas, so she rubbed it through my underwear. And when I told her about that Trojan in my wallet, she gave me a sly grin that made my legs totter.

It don't seem right to explain what happened next. I'll just say I got the ride of my life. And when we was done, as I sort of held her on that rug, Ramona went, "Pug can't know about this. No one can."

"Don't worry," I told her. "I don't tell Mom nothing."

"I just don't want her to know, that's all."

We had that white robe placed across us. My clothes were bunched under our necks like a pillow. I kissed her earlobe, then said, "All I know is—after being with you—I don't care anymore—"

But she just shook her head at me, saying, "No, Willy, no—you can't—"

So I cut in with, "No, wait! You need to listen—since I first saw you—I mean, all I think about is you—all I think about is wanting to be with you—"

And her face got all somber. Her eyes sort of fixed on my eyes. She went, "Willy—it was real nice what happened—I'll say that. I don't know why it happened, it just did—you're a wonderful boy—"

"I'm not a boy! And I want to be with you! What's wrong about that?"

Then she was playing with the hair on my forehead, sort of twirling it on a fingertip. "You are wonderful, Willy. I mean that—but what you're saying—it just won't work—"

And I guess I knew what she was getting at, but that didn't bother me none. I said, "What is it?"

Ramona kind of recoiled. She unwrapped my hair from her finger. Then her face got all bewildered. "I don't know why people do things, or don't do things—but things with me is just what they are—and I don't know if I can change them now—"

I told her, "Yeah, but I can change them for you. I really can. Trust me. I'm going places." And even though that sounded sort of corny, I meant it. I guess she knew I meant it too, because she just puckered her lips and gave me a long kiss that said, "I love you, Willy."

Then she dug around in that robe and found a pack of Pall Malls and a lighter. And I watched as she got a couple of those cigarettes stuck in her mouth. So I took that lighter and touched the flame to those coffin nails like I was some old-timey movie star or someone. Then she went, "Here you go," practically shoving one of them cigarettes in my face.

"I don't smoke."

"Well, dammit, Willy," she said, "you shouldn't have let me wasted it. What'd you think I was going to do, smoke them at the same time?"

"I don't know."

So then she hauled off and did one of the most insane things I've ever seen—she got both them cancer sticks together in her jaw like they was a single smoke. Then she just puffed all easy, real casual, sending three or four wobbly rings toward the ceiling.

"Do that again," I said, and she did.

Then she knocked some ash to the floor, telling me, "In Las Vegas, there's a guy who'll pay you a thousand dollars if you can blow one ring right through another."

"You ever done it?"

"You think I'd be here if I could?"

And though I hate everything about cigarettes, I must say there's something kind of beautiful about Ramona's manner of smoking. Her lips get all slim and delicate. The smoke slides from her sort of gradual at first, curling past her nose, then she whistles it away in a smooth stream. Then her eyelids blink a bit lazy as she takes in another breath. It's downright sexy. When she smokes, it's like she's in some distant land or something, or maybe floating outside her body. It's like all the crap that eats at her gets shaped into a circle and blown across the room.

And before I fell asleep, she finished the last cigarette in the pack. I even lit it for her. She was propped on an elbow. I was on my back looking at her. And if she'd had another box of Pall Malls, I might've stayed awake just to watch her inhale again as I fired up that lighter near her chin.

Hanna is bawling like mad. She's going, "I don't know what's wrong! What's happened to you? We can't break up now! I've never been with anybody else! I don't want to be with no one else! I'd die if I didn't have you to go with, Willy! I'd just die! I mean, I'd die if I had to go to anything by myself like—" And it's like she can't say no more because she's crying so hard.

I mean, I'm supposed to reach over and comfort her or something, but I just don't want to. And now I don't know why I bothered to go get her in the first place. To be honest, I ain't so sure I can ever explain to her about Ramona. Anyway, nothing's easy with Hanna. Nothing will be, I think. If it ain't tears, then it's yap yap yap, or it's pouty lips, or it's, "I'm sorry. Do you hate me?" A guy just gets weary of all that.

"Willy," she says, wiping her face with that tissue, "I need to be home." Then she sniffles. Then she cries some more. Then she goes, "Maybe we should talk when you know what it is you want."

"You're right," I tell her.

Then I crank the truck, switch on the headlights, and those

stupid cows panic. They go tearing off from where they came, bellowing and bashing through mesquite trees. And I figure they'll just end up by the gate that freed them, waiting for some cowboy to chase them on into their grazing pasture.

Linsteads

Joel gave me this empty notebook he found in the closet so I could write notes or draw pictures if I got bored, and Stump took that prehistoric black-and-white TV from his trailer and hooked it up by the foot of my bunk. Mom got me all these cushions to prop myself on while I play video games or watch some old movie or something. Hell, Joel even borrowed an insane video game from his pal Chubby called *Boogerman, A Pick and Flick Adventure*. Go figure. But I've had just the greatest fun running Mr. Boogerman through the Flatulent Swamps. I've been grabbing plungers for points. I've collected cans of beans for the gas meter. I've jumped, pushed, flicked, loogied, burped, super-burped, ducked, farted, super-farted, flown, dug, swung, and butt-whomped against Flying Goblins, Nose Slugs, Pus Creatures, even the Abdominal Sewer Man.

And Mom's doted on me all day, bringing me pineapple pizza slices and Coke and always asking if there's anything else I need. And from my spot here in bed I heard her vacuuming in the living room. And Joel said she was washing dishes earlier. It's like she's a whole other Mom now that I'm cut.

I guess I'm being looked after pretty well. I mean, Coach Bud stopped by this morning to check on my condition. He dumped a pile of *Sports Illustrated* magazines in bed with me. Then he mentioned that no one at school knew a thing about what had happened. He thought it was better for everyone to believe I've got some virus or something. "No need to start a mess of gossip," he said.

The thing is, not even Coach Bud has an honest idea of the

situation. Mom hardly does. But I could tell he was hoping I'd just pour my heart out to him, but I don't think I want to. He went, "I figure something fairly rough went down yesterday. You're probably not ready to discuss it. But if you need someone to talk with, I'm a phone call away. You should know that."

And before he left, he ruffled my hair like I was a kid, going, "We're going to take care of business with Jayton Friday. So you get rested. The team ain't shit without you there."

Then Doc came over around noon. He changed my bandage and checked the wound. He said it wasn't bad at all. He told me I'd be fine for Friday's game, but I'd have to be careful of the stitches. He said, "As long as your gut's wrapped good, you'll be okay," which made me feel a ton better.

To be truthful, I'm lucky. I lost my head last night. Just lost it. And that's how I found myself on Doc's examining table. Forget that I'd left a path of blood all the way from Amarillo to Claude, from the lobby of the Royal Hotel to the backseat of Mom's station wagon, except most of it dripped from this inch slit in my midsection. And I was almost naked on that table, and Doc was pulling gauze around my belly, saying, "Thank God it didn't get deep enough to nick at any of the vitals—but it's an ugly cut—it's ugly—"

Not much was going through my mind then. Just emptiness. My clothes were in a pile on the floor. My Wranglers and western shirt and T-shirt had these dark stains on them that showed more black than red. Mom was across the office sort of weeping by herself. And Coach Bud was there too, though I don't know how he got the news so quick. I mean, Jesus, it was late and everyone just seemed all dramatic and upset. Except me. I wasn't feeling nothing.

Then Coach Bud stepped in next to Doc, and they both appeared uncombed from sleep. And Coach Bud's face just wrinkled with emotion. "Will he be able to go, Doc? Can he play with it—?"

But Doc didn't say a word. He just shrugged. And that's

when Mom began her hollering. She went right after Coach Bud, sort of jostled him once or twice with her palms, going, "No! No more! Nothing else is going to happen to him!"

I'd never seen Coach Bud come close to being scared before, but the way his face crinkled with Mom's voice and hands made him look like some stupid dog after it'd been kicked in the ribs a few times. He just cowered away from the table, his eyes shooting from me to her to Doc, saying, "I didn't mean—I—that's not how I meant it—" but I don't think none of us believed him for a second.

Then Mom just covered her face with those shoving palms. She kind of began vibrating some. And when Coach Bud went to put an arm around her, she just fell into him all sobby with, "He's my boy, Bud."

And afterwards, as Mom was driving us home, I sat there all amazed on how things change so fast. And even though it'd been only a few hours since I'd come home from school to find Junie and Bob standing at the front door, it seemed more like months. They were all dressed fancy for a night on the town, and Junie smiled at me, going, "Hi, handsome!"

And Bob went, "Hey, hoss."

So I said, "Hi, guys."

Junie patted my shoulder all sweet, saying, "I used your shower again. Me and Bob are heading to the Pork Barrel dance in Sweetwater."

"Mom gone?"

"She's serving in Amarillo tonight."

"Where's Joel?"

"Spending the night at Chubby's—so we're out of here. You got the place to yourself for once."

"Have fun," I told them.

"We will," Bob said. Then he went, "Hang in there, hoss."

"Bye, hon."

Then the screen door whapped behind them, and I crossed on over to the couch and collapsed. Then I listened as Bob's sedan pulled from the drive. And I was getting kind of restless. I had Ramona on my brain. And Hanna was there too, because I was feeling sort of bad for ignoring her today. She'd tried talking to me twice, once at lunch, the other between fourth and fifth period, but I wasn't too responsive. "Call tonight," she finally said.

"Okay."

"You promise?"

"We'll see."

I lifted from that couch. Then I went to the TV, but I guess I wasn't too interested because I didn't bother switching it on. I just stood there gawking at the blank screen. Then I turned on the heels of my boots and surveyed the living room. Empty Coors cans. Dairy Mart cups. Some of Mom's clothes in a heap on the recliner. A mess of newspapers on the floor by Joel's Nerf football.

Next thing I knew, my fingers were punching Hanna's number on the telephone. Then ol' Waylon's voice boomed from the receiver with, "Lockhart!"

So I went, "Is Hanna there?" But I said that all high and different, hoping he might figure it was someone else.

And he didn't say nothing for a moment. Then I heard him calling, "Hanna!"

And when she got on the line, I mumbled, "It's me."

"Willy! I just knew you'd call! Listen, we can see each other tonight, and I know how it's been lately, but it'll be okay! I'll get Daddy to let us go out a little bit tonight! We can go over to the Mart! Everybody'll be there, and then we'll have some time before I need to be in!" It about drove me nuts. She just kept rambling and yapping. She said, "I know I can be bitchy, but I don't mean to be. I've written almost six poems this afternoon about you. One's called 'Morning Glory,' then there's 'Sweetness, Hello' and 'How It Was When It Was' and 'Things I Wish He'd Say,' and I haven't named the other two yet." She just wouldn't shut up. I was biting my lip all hard. And it's like the more she chattered, the more I wanted to be with Ramona. In fact, I was getting sort of tense. My left hand was practically choking that phone to death, while my right worked at stretching the coils from the cord. And as she went, "I know that Lee and Sammy and—" I lowered that receiver from my ear. Then I hung up the phone. And the house seemed real quiet then, almost peaceful. It was already getting dusky outside. And I knew she was bound to call back, so I grabbed a Coke from the fridge and got the hell out of there.

I guess I imagined Ramona would be all happy at the sight of me. She'd open her door and go, "Willy!" Then she'd tug my body into that room like she'd done the other night. But that ain't what she did at all. Instead she went, "What are you doing? You can't—" And she was fixed all clean and beautiful. She wore a short skirt. She had on those red pumps. Her face was painted like a model or someone, but her expression showed shock.

I said, "I got to see you—I—" Then I tried to step past the doorway, but she put a hand on my chest.

"You can't come in now!"

So I sort of leaned toward her, going, "Ramona—"

But she wouldn't have it. She got pretty uptight then. She almost yelled, "No, Willy! You can't!"

"What's wrong?"

"Please go! Now!"

"But I want to see you!"

"No! I'm leaving in a second! I got to go, and you got to leave!"

And it hurt like a sonofabitch. It just tore at my insides. "I—I want to talk—I—"

But Ramona just shook her head. Then she shouted real angry. "Oh God," she went, "just get away from here! I don't need this now! Leave me alone!"

Then she gave me a final push and slammed the door, and I just stood there for a while like a fool, going, "What'd I do? What'd I do?"

And this is where it all gets jumbled in my head. I still can't piece it all together really. I was heading through the lobby. I kept thinking, "Fucking shit." Then over and over again I started grumbling those words to myself because I couldn't figure nothing out. "Fucking shit. Fucking shit." And that *Penthouse*-reading-jazz-liking-veiny-eyed clerk gave me a harsh glance from behind his desk. I mean, if he hadn't been so big and all, I'd have cracked his skull plumb apart then. I'd have pounded him against that desktop until his face busted all wide and gross. Man, I'm sure as hell glad I didn't do that now.

Anyway, I was about to say something unclever to that clerk like, "Go screw yourself," or, "Take a picture, it'll last longer," when I heard this woman's voice just babbling nearby. She was saying, "You know what my friend Lucy says, Graham—it ain't what money does for you—wait, that ain't it—"

I swung around, then I just froze. It was like my whole body had sunk into tar or something. Mom was ambling out of Roughnecks with some older fellow in a business suit. She had her arm looped in his arm. Even though it was winter and all, she had on this tight blouse I'd never seen before, as well as this black skirt. She was talking and talking, but I couldn't hear a thing pouring from her mouth. And what's really weird is that she didn't seem to recognize me at first. There they were, no more than ten feet away, strolling in my direction, but I might as well have been somebody else's kid.

Everything kind of breaks down in my memory here.

I hollered, "What are you doing?"

Mom jerked her head up. Business Suit stopped in his steps. Then Mom went, "Willy? What in God's name—"

"What are you doing here?"

Business Suit got pretty uncomfortable then. "Who is this?" His look shot from me to Mom to me to Mom.

"Oh, God, Willy—did you follow me?"

That desk clerk eased from his stool.

This is what I wrote this morning in that notebook Joel gave me. This is how I tried to make some sense of what happened. It's all so quick and cluttered, but this is what I got on paper before Coach Bud stopped by after breakfast:

I'm yelling like a maniac at Mom.

Ramona comes down the stairs. But I don't see her yet.

I'm going off on Mom because I don't understand why she's there with Business Suit who is nervous and not happy about what I'm saying.

Desk Clerk is moving around the desk.

Mom: Calm down Willy, just calm down for a sec!

Then Ramona is there.

Ramona is there with the same two guys I'd seen in Roughnecks the other night. Mr. Polyester Slacks. Biker Guy.

I lose control.

I'm pointing at Mr. PS.

Me: Is this your greasy bastard Ramona, is this him?

Mr. PS: Who the fuck are you?

Is that him? This the dirty bastard?

Ramona appears frightened.

Mom appears frightened.

Business Suit puts a hand on my shoulder: Son.

I ain't his son.

Ramona: Willy.

Mr. PS is in my face: Hey, what the fuck you doin anyhow?

Biker Guy stands by Ramona.

Mom goes toward me.

I fling an arm at her.

I send her stumbling back.

I don't mean to push her that hard.

Mr. PS grabs my shirt.

Me: Fuck you!

Hey, you fuckin don't talk to me like that!

I throw a heavy punch into PSs face.

Blood spurts from PSs nose.

PS drops to the lobby floor.

Biker Guy jumps at me.

I swing wild like crazy.

A punch catches BG on the side of the head.

One of BGs arms swings up into my stomach.

Mom and Ramona are screaming.

I'm grabbing my stomach.

My shirt is turning red.

Blood spreads between my fingers.

The blood is warm.

Business Suit to BG: Good lord!!!

BG is holding a pocket knife.

BG is nodding his head at me.

BG is walking backwards from me.

BG touches his ear where I hit him.

BG is heading toward me again.

Desk Clerk is suddenly there.

DC is bellowing over the crying and screaming of Mom and Ramona.

DC to BG: Stay put!!!

I don't remember what I'm doing now.

Business Suit is pale.

Business Suit is shaking his head.

Business Suit takes off running out of the hotel.

BG glares at DC.

DC is at my side.

I fly at BG.

Mom and DC hold me back.

Now I'm on my knees.

Mom is nuts.

Mom is on her knees too.

Mom is trying to see where the blood is coming from.

BG is furious.

BGs teeth are clinched.

BG is coming at me again.

BG to me: You little fucker!!!

DC gets in front of BG.

DC to BG: Walk away!!! NOW!!!

PS is rolling around on the floor with a hand over his nose.

Ramona is heading up the stairs.

Ramona is carrying on and on.

DC says to Mom: Get him out of here lady, get the boy some help!!!

It wasn't like the movies at all. I mean, a guy gets stabbed and he's supposed to just slump and die. Or if he doesn't die, then he kind of sits there waiting for death. But I couldn't stay still in Mom's station wagon. I was twisting all over the place, except I wasn't squirming from pain or the bleeding. To be truthful, the only pain I had going on then was inside my brain. I was somewhere between mad and sad about Ramona. I was stretched in the back-seat, my shirt all sticky and damp, mumbling, "Goddammit—"

Mom hauled us from Amarillo to Claude at the speed of light. She must've ran a billion red lights. She tried acting brave for me, but I could hear her sniffling and all. She kept saying, "Hang in there, baby," and, "How you doing?" Then she turned on the radio. But soon a song kicked in with, "When your heart is aching—" so I told her to switch the station.

And after she'd gone and woke Doc, after I'd got all stitched and everything, I found myself in bed. I had my eyes shut. Mom had tucked these quilts around me. She was cross-legged on the floor, sort of rubbing the palm on one of my hands. Her head rested on the edge of the bed near my chest. She said how proud she was of me. How good a football player I am. She said she appreciated all I'd done for Joel. Her voice sounded all tired and hoarse. Then she said nothing for a little while, and I thought she was falling asleep or something. Then she went, "I never told you much about the Linsteads—about the Linstead family—but before you were ever born, everybody in King County knew them—or at least knew about them. The daddy of the family was Harp Linstead—Harp Linstead was a rodeo cowboy when he was young—some said as good as there was in Texas—but by the time his kids started growing up, he was all busted up—walked with a limp. He worked the ranches long as he could, then he had to work at farming or over at the gin—he—he just couldn't stand that—started drinking all the time—and fighting. He'd go home all bloody and drunk—and then cry because he just couldn't do right by his family."

So I just listened. And it was like I wasn't even around. She just seemed to be talking to herself, saying, "There were six kids at the old place—three girls and three boys—and the girls were about as pretty as any around, I guess, and the boys were handsome in their own ways—but the thing was—the boys—they started it too—drinking and getting in fights over in Lubbock or Childress or places like that—and it got to where people were afraid of the Linsteads—even the police—and then some real bad things happened—and two of the boys—they got sent to prison off in Huntsville—the other one, he just left and never came back—and for the girls—people just don't know what it was like—with brothers in prison—a daddy always drunk—there were plenty of boys who wanted to take them out, but they were afraid to— so by the time the girls were in their teens, the only men after them were drillers—roughnecks—cowboys. Two of the girls got married and then there was just the baby girl left at home—and while the daddy kept drinking and fighting and getting old and awfully pitiful, the mama—she just somehow put up with it all—she'd sit in her chair and read the Bible—she'd keep reading over and over that part that says, 'for everybody has sinned and come short of the glory of God.' Anyhow, this last girl at home, she got to be seventeen—and she met—I met—your daddy. It was when oil was big and they were drilling out east. He was so big and strong— not afraid of anything—we'd drink and dance all night and then go over to the Caprock to watch the sun come up. For the first time I could forget about being one of the Linstead girls. Your daddy made me laugh and feel pretty and—he'd act real proud of me. I'd sleep in the backseat of his car and wait on him when he was out working midnight shifts—then one night we got married by a JP over at Ardmore—all I could think was, I'd never be a Linstead again. I never went back until after Harp Linstead died—then later Mama died—then you came along and Joel came along—but somehow things just didn't seem to work right—the oil played out—we moved to Shamrock—things got pretty bad—then we moved to Claude—and one day your dad and I had a big fight—and he left."

And she got kind of weepy at that point. Too many people crying these days, I thought. But Mom didn't let those tears stop her none, she just continued with, "Stump was around. He helped us out. Somehow the years got by—all I ever really wanted was for you and Joel to go to school like most kids are supposed to—to go on real dates—someday be in one of them gowns that you graduate in—with pictures of you in a class—so—"

I glanced at her. She squeezed my hand once, shaking her head all roughly. She said, "It's a real job I have in Amarillo—Mr. Graham, who you saw me with tonight, he gave me a real job—and he's treated us good, Willy—it's just that some time back—with his wife like she is and everything—sometimes him and me—you know—but, Willy, I swear it's not what it looked like—I guess I know it's not right, but the one thing I know is that I do love you and Joel. No matter what else. I just never learned how to act like it—or to say it like I should—but you and Joel are the only good things that ever happened to me—ever—all I want in this world right now is that you know that—you and Joel—"

Then she just bawled and bawled. So I took her fingers from my palm and moved my arms around her shoulders. I pulled her real close. Then I bent some to give her a kiss on the forehead. I didn't know what to say, but I wished I'd said something. Truthfully, nothing felt real anymore.

So now Joel and I are here in bed together watching this old movie on Stump's TV. Joel is pressed against me. We got a bowl of trail mix between us. The movie is about these Japanese samurai fellows who are protecting some village from outlaws. There are subtitles, which makes it kind of hard to follow.

"Willy—?" Joel says.

"It ain't nothing," I tell him.

And I keep imagining what I'd be like as one of them samurais. I guess I'd be fairly good and all. Except samurais don't cry, I think.

Javelina Fears

I've never seen a night so bright. Or if I have, I just don't remember. There's about a billion trillion stars. The moon is full and huge and sort of yellowish, and that man up there is looking down on me, saying, "You done good, Willy, bunged knee and stitches and all, you done good." And I couldn't have said it better myself.

I ain't so sure how many Coors I've had, but I'm not feeling nothing. And I wasn't feeling nothing when I played tonight either. Coach Bud had me change in his office so the team wouldn't spot the padding around my stitches, and while I was still in my Jockeys, Doc gave me a couple of pokes with this syringe. Hello, bandage, how about a needle? There now. That wasn't so bad. But I couldn't help flinching like a baby, because I don't like needles one bit. They remind me too much of T.K.'s cattle, and I ain't a cow. But whatever was in that syringe had me fine and dandy by first whistle.

Anyway, the game ain't worth much of a mention, other than to say the bleachers supported almost every ass in Claude. Those two scouts were there also. They had their clipboards on their laps, and after the fourth quarter, once we'd trounced Jayton, Coach Bud took me aside and introduced that pair as Mr. Meredith and Mr. Dignetti.

"Pretty impressive stuff tonight," is what that black scout said as he shook my hand, but I forget if he was Meredith or Dignetti.

Then that white fellow went, "We'd like to find a time to sit down and chat with you, Willy."

And I said exactly what Coach Bud had told me to: "Just talk to Coach here, he'll set everything up."

By then I was all excited inside because it was a great night for the Tigers. We just rolled, jumped, pounded, and dumped all over those Jayton Javelinas. No problem. I mean, there I was before the game all wired and bothered on the bench, just being moody and scanning the field. Then I spotted Burgess Lefcourt, #44, that husky, hulking middle-backer, sitting on the opposing bench. He had on a hard, mean grimace, like he was hurting or something. Then his eyes found me. And I figured right away what was going on in his brain. "Dead man on the Tigers' bench," that's what he was thinking. "Dead man."

So I leaned on over to Harvey, saying, "Early on—that big middle-backer—let him come clean."

Harvey got all surprised. He about squawked, "Let him?"

"I need to beat him early."

And Harvey stared at me with this puzzled expression, then he shrugged. Then he said, "You sure?"

"Yeah."

And this is how it played with #44:

We trotted to the line. Lee barked out the signals, then he handed me the ball. I went forward with a power-run, gaining some four or five yards. Then KABLAM! Me and Burgess had collided like a couple of rams or something. My legs churned with the impact, but I bulled on ahead. I swear to God, Burgess couldn't stop me from coming. Next thing I knew, he was falling. Then he grappled with my thigh some. Then he slipped the tackle altogether, and I left him on the ground. That's when I gained another twenty yards before being dog-piled by four of the Javelinas' secondary defensive players. And even though I got clobbered fairly good, I knew I was locked in the Zone for the rest of the game.

Harvey, Lee, and Sammy were there slapping me on the helmet as I climbed to my feet. Coach Bud had a shit-eating smile. Coach Slick was clapping his hands, going, "That a boy!" Mr.

Dignetti and Mr. Meredith jotted notes like crazy. Those bleachers sighed with relief as those butts lifted off them. Even Hanna and the cheerleaders were kicking higher than usual. From then on, Mr. Burgess Lefcourt practically dropped to the grass before I reached him. And after the game, as everyone made nice with each other on the field, Burgess came over to where I was at. He gave me this firm shake. He went, "You got me, man. My fucking shoulder is killing me."

My head is buzzing like a motherfucker. My body is flushed and warm. This wintery weather just can't reach the Coors in my blood. And, Jesus Christ, it's so beautiful here. I'm gazing plumb into infinity, all twinkle and black and twinkle. I'm blowing steam past my lips. I'm giving that man in the moon a wink. And there's music coming from the house.

> Did you ever see Dallas from a DC-9 at night?
> Well, Dallas is a jewel
> Oh yeah, Dallas is a beautiful sight
> And Dallas is a jungle
> But Dallas gives a beautiful light
> Have you ever seen Dallas from a DC-9 at night?

I can hear the others too. Stump is yelling for Mom to put more ice in the cooler. Bob is laughing at something with Junie. Lee's going, "Where'd he go?"

And Sammy is saying, "If we're doing quarters, we need Willy!"

But the party is almost over, nearly everyone has hit the road, so I'm keeping to myself now. I'm hiding near the porch, sort of crouched in the darkness on one side of the house. And I'm thinking about what Joel told me before I played tonight. I'd come from the shower with a towel around my waist. He was on the floor by the bunk. He had this book in his lap. I said, "Tell me something, Joel."

He went, "Every breath you take, you inhale a single molecule of air that Julius Caesar exhaled the second he croaked."

"Imagine that," I said, kind of dabbing a towel edge on the purple and blue skin circling my stitches. I mean, ain't that the damnedest thing. Just now, Caesar goes in, someone else goes out, or something like that. For all I know, I'm sucking in a little Hitler, maybe some Jesus, not to mention a whole ton of folks I don't even know of.

"Hey, you out here?"

Someone's on the porch. The screen door smacked shut. Then the boards sort of went CREEEEAAAAK. Sammy whispers, "Willy?" Then he goes, "Willy!"

"Sorry, Sammy," my mind says, "but I'm getting all cozy with the universe. I'll be in in a minute."

Then the boards CREEEEAAAAK some more. The screen door whaps. And Sammy's inside going, "Is he in the bathroom? Hey, Willy, you in there, man?"

And Joel shouts, "It's me!" And suddenly everyone's giggling and carrying on like drunken maniacs.

To be truthful, it wasn't much of a party, but Mom wanted to throw one anyway. "Because I'm so damn proud of you," was how she explained it. Besides, Stump and Bob made a bundle from betting on the game, so I guess they figured a party in my honor was the right thing to do. Still, Coach Bud stopped by for a few beers, so did Sheriff Branches, who got so gone on wine coolers that me and Bob had to help him across the drive to his patrol car.

Coach Slick and Jackie showed up with their cameras. But Mom didn't want them taking any pictures because she said the house wasn't clean. That didn't stop Coach Slick, though. He got a great shot of me spraying beer on Sammy. Then Jackie had me and Lee and Sammy get together with Coach Slick, then he took four or five pictures of us all being goofy—

Sammy giving Coach Slick rabbit ears, while I did the same to Lee.

Coach Slick getting me in a headlock. Sammy and Lee holding their fists like they was about to smash my ribs.

Sammy puckering his lips at Lee. Lee puckering his lips at me. My face covered. Coach Slick having rabbit ear revenge on Sammy.

Then me and Lee and Sammy hopping on Coach Slick's back, but I'd wished we hadn't done that. I mean, I'm sure the picture will be funny and all, but Coach Slick's got this whompy knee from his football days. He was grinning, saying, "Careful, guys." Then he had to go sit on the couch for a spell, and I knew we'd thrown too much weight on him.

Anyway, Tamla arrived later and brought a great chocolate cake she'd made, but she didn't stay around too long. Of course, Hanna didn't come. Neither did Ramona, but I guess Mom hadn't invited her or anything.

As far as Hanna goes, well, that's done with. She gave me this note at school yesterday that went:

Willy,
  I'm so sorry it has come to this. It is clear to me that you no longer feel the need to talk to me. I don't understand, but you have some growing up to do. After talking with my parents and Mrs. Christian, I think we should have a break from each other. If you want to talk to me, I will listen. But I can no longer be left out in the cold by your childish way of acting. I will always love you, but I think it would be better for both of us if we saw other people. I hope we can be friends.

Hanna

I mean, what she wrote would've torn up a mess of other guys, but I was so happy I nearly screamed, "Hallelujah!" Then earlier this evening, Lee had me step outside with him. He was already drunk, but I noticed he was all serious and anxious about something. He said, "Willy, we been friends since we was kids, so I needed to ask you. And I'm asking you because I'm not a rotten son of a bitch, or some back-stabbing bastard, or any of that."

"Hell, I know that."

"You don't know that! Now just hold on!" I mean, Lee was so nervous that he hardly made a lick of sense. Then he went, "You and Hanna were sweethearts for some time."

"That's true."

"And I know she means a lot to you."

"I guess, Lee."

"It's just that me and Patricia—you know. And you and Hanna—the same. So I was wondering—"

"Ain't a problem," I told him.

"Now don't say that yet, Willy. I'm just asking. The last thing I'd want to do is ruin my friendship with you. There ain't a woman on the planet that I'd let do that. I swear to God. I swear to God."

So we walked to the end of the porch for a pee, and I said, "Hell, Lee, if anyone's going to be with Hanna besides me, then I'd want it to be someone I knew would treat her right."

"You know I'd do that. You know it."

And when we was done pissing our business, I gave Lee this monster hug. We just stood there for the longest time like that—my arms around him, his arms around me. Then he said, "I'm freezing," and back inside we went, smiling and joking like we always do, ambling toward that big cooler on the living room floor.

I don't know much about stars, except for what Joel has mentioned. There are stars that are dying. There are stars getting born too. Some stars are bigger than anything in this galaxy, I think. Then there's stars that ain't around no more, but a guy can still spot them shining up there. I don't understand that.

The thing is, if it weren't for that bunch inside playing quarters and hollering and playing music and everything, it'd be real easy for me to imagine I was in the sky there. That'd be something. The Willy star, floating in the universe, just twink twink twinkling.

Mr. Man in the Moon goes, "You're drunk, son."

"Mr. Man in the Moon," I tell him, "no offense, fuck you."

That's what Lee used to say, but not exactly. He'd go, "Hey, Willy, see the windshield wiper?"

"Yeah."

"Fuck the windshield wiper."

"See Waylon Lockhart, fuck Waylon Lockhart."

But that was a while ago, and he don't say that no more. That was when we'd sneak out to T.K.'s ranch in the middle of the night. We was maybe fourteen or fifteen then. It was summer. Sometimes we'd take a dip in the Maitlands' pool, but mostly we went to the pen where T.K. kept this wild boar he'd caught. That had to be about the meanest pig I've ever encountered in my life. Soon as we kneeled at the fence, that pig would come charging. It'd snort and bellow, then WHAM! The sucker would crash its dumb skull into the metal rails just trying to get at us.

"See that pig?"

"Yeah."

"Fuck that pig."

Lee and I had a game too. We'd take turns climbing into that pen, then we'd haul ass from one end to the other. Psycho boar would come tearing. SQUEAL! SNORT! EEEEEEEEEE! We'd jump into the next pen, spooking the sheep, and then we'd do it again.

That was the same summer that me and Lee went camping in the Caprock. And we'd stretch across our sleeping bags and gaze right into this very same sky. And sometimes we'd tell ghost stories, or we'd just make up shit about people. And what I never told Lee or no one else is that I used to get sort of creeped out there. I'd imagine that boar getting loose. Then he'd be searching for me and Lee. I guess it seems pretty stupid now, but it about drove me nuts then. Anyway, like I said, that was a while ago, and now we're older. And, hell, Lee's just about the best guy I know, aside from Sammy. It don't bug me at all him wanting to be with Hanna. Not at all. And soon as everything calms down with Ramona, once I get where I'm going, I'll tell him everything. I'll show him and Sammy my scar. I'll explain about all that stuff in Amarillo. It'll be a big laugh.

"See the moon, Lee, fuck the moon!"

And now I'm thinking Claude will soon be a distant recollection. Come next fall, this town and this house and all those people inside won't be seeing me around much, and I can't imagine getting back here too often. In a way, I'm already saying goodbye to high school and my small-town football life. And I'm not so sure where exactly I'll be in a year, but I know it'll be good. It'll be great.

So this is the end of my story. Sure, I probably won't encounter Ramona again, and I don't expect to. Maybe she'll get some nice job in a café or something. Maybe she'll find someone to treat her right, someone who'll light up them Pall Malls and blow a little smoke ring right through a big one. But as corny as it sounds, I'll keep on thinking about her until she just disappears from my mind. I swear, whenever I spot some woman walking toward me on a sidewalk, or sitting close by on a bus or something, I'll glance at her just in case I might catch Ramona's dark, tired eyes. And like Mom, she's got plenty of time to make a difference for herself. I mean, she's not that old. But the truth is, if I've learned anything it's this—one soul can't really save another. The best thing to do is take care of yourself, be decent, keep running forward. That's what I aim to do. That's about the only thing I know for sure.

What else can I mention about myself at this very moment? I got a ton of ambition and my future is about as bright as those stars overhead. In a weird way, it's not like I've got much influence in it. It's like everything is just fixed and unchanging, like the Willy book was written before I was born and all I have to do is play the part. All the same, I can't think of a better ending than where I am tonight. I mean, who doesn't like a success story? And in a way, I'm sure everyone concerned will get what they want: Hanna a new boyfriend; Waylon rid of me; Sammy college; Coach Bud respect for him and the team; Joel a bedroom of his own; Dad a car with plenty of gas and a babe riding shotgun; Jackie happiness; Ramona the memory of a kid who fell in love with the idea of loving her; Mom a son making her proud even when things seem hard; and Claude a hero.

So now I'm inhaling all the air I can. And I got this amazing thought. I mean, even when I get blue and start missing everybody, all I got to do is take me a big ol' breath, and those molecules are going to be there. It's like carrying around a piece of hair or something, or how I keep that rhinestone hairclip with me all the time, but different. Take a deep breath. Hi, Mom. Hey, Joel. How you doing, Dad? Hello, Ramona. It's like, if everybody in the world knew about that, no one would be lonely or nothing. And that's just about the damnedest thing I can think of.

About the Author

Mitch Cullin's fiction has been published in *Christopher Street* and other magazines. Besides being widely anthologized, his work has won various awards, including the 1996 Sylvan Karchmer Short Story Award, the 1997 Charles Oliver Memorial Award for Fiction, and the 6th Annual Stony Brook Short Fiction Prize. He lives in Tucson, Arizona.

WHOMPYJAWED

DISCUSSION POINTS

1. Consider the opening paragraph in *Whompyjawed*. What does it reveal about the narrator's age or character? What does it reveal about the town? What kind of tone does it set for the story that follows?

2. Pick a couple of sentences from Willy's narration. Examine Mitch Cullin's language and the overall style of the writing throughout *Whompyjawed*. Through his choice of words, tone, and often repeated phrases, how does Cullin reveal Willy's character? Is Willy a reliable narrator? How do others see Willy? How does Cullin make Willy a sympathetic character? How would this story work if he had portrayed him otherwise?

3. Discuss Mitch Cullin's creative chapter format throughout *Whompyjawed*. Does the format do a good job of reflecting the thought processes of the teenage storyteller? What are some of the other ways that the author makes this an effective coming-of-age story?

4. Cullin uses the word *whompyjawed* about six times in the book. What significant events occur each time it's used? What does the word mean to you? How does *whompyjawed* apply to Willy's story? Why is it an appropriate word for the book's title?

5. Explore the theme of football and competition in Willy's life and future. How does his view of himself as player/hero, garnered from his narration and interior monologues, compare to how others see him? Why does everyone expect Willy to play after he's been stabbed? Why does the coach want to hide the stabbing from the other players?

6. What is Willy really being groomed for? What, if any, is another career path that Willy could pursue?

7. How realistically does the author handle Willy's emerging sexuality? What is the significance of the football star's first sexual encounter with Jackie, a boy, and why does Mitch Cullin make this a part of Willy's story? Do you think this is a typical experience for boys—a run-of-the-mill adolescent rite of passage? Why? What makes Willy so enamored with Ramona, and what turns him off to Hanna?

8. Examine the roles of the other characters in Willy's life, especially his philosophical little brother, Joel; his mother, Pug; his coach, Bud; Coach Slick; and Ramona. How do they further the story and the reader's understanding of Willy's life?

9. Consider the mind-bending facts that Joel spouts to Willy, like "Every breath you take, you inhale a single molecule of air that Julius Caesar exhaled the second he croaked." Is their timing significant to the story? How do they fit into the story as a whole?

10. Why does Willy choose John Wayne as his alter ego? How does it further the reader's understanding of how Willy views himself?

11. How did you feel at the point in the book when Willy, while with Ramona, discovers his mother outside the bar and gets stabbed? Then examine his mother's monologue about her life. What effect do these events have on Willy, considering the biggest game of his life is imminent? Why is the mother's story important to include here?

12. Explore the significance of the opening quote by Jean-Paul Sartre. Discuss its meaning in terms of Willy's story in *Whompyjawed*.

NOTE FROM THE AUTHOR

For almost two years I struggled to write this novel. In hindsight, I attribute my difficulty to the book's generally simple language, which is so at odds with my innate verbosity. Still, the story had elements that I loved exploring—a character sensing profundity in his life but somehow unable to fully articulate it, people's frequent need to feed off of and manipulate other individuals, and how we can carry incredible hopefulness when no hope is readily apparent. With that in mind, I think *Whompyjawed* is a very American book, and I think Willy Keeler represents the best and worst qualities in most of us. More than anything, that was what compelled me to write his story.